ROBYN

A CHRISTMAS BRIDE

JACQUI NELSON

Cover design by Erin Dameron-Hill

ISBN eBook: 978-0-9958596-5-4
ISBN Print: 978-0-9958596-4-7

PRAISE FOR THE NOELLE, CHRISTMAS STORIES...

The Calling Birds
Noelle, Colorado - Christmas 1876

"Jack and Birdie's story is suspenseful, romantic, sweet story of family, trust, love and survival. I couldn't put this story down!" ~ Carter and Conners Mom

"With secrets, outlaws, greed, and love this all provides for an amazing adventure." ~ Sandra S.

"An unforgettable read. Lovable characters, page turning plot, and satisfying resolution to all kinds of conflicts." ~ Deutsche OMA

"Birdie is a delight sassy woman who knows how to stand her ground...I loved the humor, the fear, the race against time" ~ Cyn

Robyn: A Christmas Bride
Noelle, Colorado - Christmas 1877

"The perfect book to set the mood for the Christmas spirit!" ~ Maria D.

"Beautiful story of friendship, love, and forever happy ever after." ~ Tonya L.

"I loved this book. It was revisiting old friends" ~ TJW

"Jacqui has hit a home run with this one!" ~ Peggy C.

DEDICATION

For Quinn and MaryAnn

CHAPTER 1

Denver, Colorado
December 21, 1877

"She's gone?" Max Peregrine shouted, disbelief then panic raising his voice to a roar. "Where?"

Lined up shoulder to shoulder inside the Denver office of Peregrines' Post and Freight, the three Llewellyn brothers studied him intently, not with surprise but curiosity. And something more. Something his careening thoughts couldn't identify.

Brynmor, the eldest by several years, heaved a sympathetic-sounding sigh. "She's—"

"Fine," Heddwyn interrupted, embracing his status as the swift-talking middle brother who needed to do everything quick, including driving freight wagons at breakneck speed. He shot his brothers a secretive glance. "Remember our plan. He sounds upset, but we need to know more."

"Stuff your plans!" Max threw down his pencil and stormed around the desk where he'd been working on his ledgers. He'd throttle his answers from Robyn's brothers if need be. "Why—did—she—leave!?"

Griffin, the youngest but also the largest, folded his arms over his barrel of a chest. "He sounds more than upset."

"Good." Standing on either side of their flame-haired baby brother, Brynmor and Heddwyn spoke and nodded in unison, like matching musclebound bookends with the same auburn hair and sky-blue eyes. Except Bryn had one eye clouded white. Max had yet to learn why.

The Llewellyns were fond of talk but notoriously unforthcoming on certain subjects. Like, at the moment, Robyn's departure.

"He's regretting something," Griffin added.

Max froze. Leave it to Griff to pinpoint Max's state of mind while never addressing his own. Griff's hair color matched his sister's, but his reputation as the Llewellyn sibling with a short fuse was his alone.

"I regret"—he unlocked his clenched jaw and tried to speak normally—"that your sister might have put herself in jeopardy."

Heddwyn snorted. "Little Red can take care of herself."

"Hedd's right. The wee one is all grown-up," Bryn proclaimed with another sigh.

"She's as tough as she is beautiful." Griff's gaze narrowed, studying him even more keenly. "Or do you believe otherwise?"

"I don't," Max muttered, thinking of Robyn's lean strength, steely blue gaze, and stunning smile. A smile he'd been blessed to see every day since he moved to Denver. A smile he craved more than a miner coveted gold. A smile that had become increasingly melancholy of late. "Whatever's wrong and wherever she's gone, she needn't be alone. I would've traveled with her."

"You sure 'bout that?" Hedd released a low whistle as he pointed at Max's face. "Look! Dog Bone's turning the same shade of red as Ruddy does when he's near to exploding."

In Welsh, *Griff* meant *ruddy,* but that hothead remained poker-faced as he said, "We have eyes, Peaceful. No need telling us something we can plainly see."

Max's entire body burned with outrage. Not because of the teasing titles the Llewellyns loved to dole out, for themselves and others. In Welsh, *Heddwyn* meant *blessed peace*, a constant source of ribbing for a man who had too much energy to stand still. Max had learned to look below the surface of their name tomfoolery after Robyn revealed her brothers called him Dog Bone because he never stopped gnawing problems into submission.

He didn't give up. A trait all of the Llewellyns found admirable. If they assigned you a name, even one you didn't find flattering, it meant you'd earned their respect. They didn't waste their time on people they didn't like.

Robyn's explanation along with her easy smile had ended his dislike for long conversations. But only with her. They'd talked about everything after that, argued as much as they'd agreed, but always ended up smiling.

No topic had been taboo, or so he thought. Why hadn't she spoken to him before she left? And how could her brothers question his resolve, especially when it came to Robyn?

Their lack of faith left him not only furious but frustrated and flummoxed. "If your sister asked, I'd have gone *anywhere* with her."

Bryn raised an eyebrow in challenge. "You said differently in the past."

"I did not."

"Did too," Hedd shot back. "Then Rob said she had to go there. No other place would do."

"Took the Clydesdale." Griff thrust his thumb over his shoulder. "In better weather, she'd be there by now."

Max's gaze leapt in the direction he'd indicated, hoping to see Robyn behind her brothers. That this was some colossal joke.

Driven by a fickle wind, his world spun faster than the snow outside the window. She couldn't be gone. Not in such a storm. Not when he needed her, when they all needed her. She was the thread that held everything together. Did her brothers seriously believe he wouldn't have accompanied her on any journey? They'd lost their minds. He couldn't do the same. He had to find Robyn.

"Where is *there*?" he asked through clenched teeth. "Tell me what she said. *Exactly*."

Griff drew in a breath that swelled his chest to even more massive proportions and said with exaggerated precision, "*I need to spread my wings and try new things.*"

"Those are my words!"

"Really?" Hedd replied with mock surprise.

"You know they are. I said them when you and Robyn swarmed me like bees on a new honeycomb asking questions about me coming to Denver to open a hub for Peregrines' Post." He'd used the same words when his family wondered why he couldn't stay with them in Noelle, the once dying but now thriving mining town high in the mountains.

A year and a half had passed. He hadn't gone back. Not even for a visit. The only family he'd seen was Birdie and Grandpa Gus. The petite mail-order bride who'd married his brother last Christmas had bundled his grandfather onto a wagon and visited him twice last summer.

He liked his sister-in-law's industrious nature and her adoration whenever she mentioned Jack. Despite them being at brotherly loggerheads, he was relieved Jack had finally found happiness with Birdie. His brother had lost more than most, both in the war and later when his first wife betrayed him.

During her visits and in her letters, Birdie always urged Max to come home. Noelle was prospering. Nearly a year ago, twelve marriages—including Birdie and Jack's—had given the town stability. The train line, promised in exchange for those unions, had been completed. Hardt's mine continued to produce silver. Despite all that good news, Noelle had its fair share of turmoil. Investing all of your time in one tiny town wasn't wise.

"Trying new things led me to Denver. My family's business had to diversify to survive. We have lots of work here. There's no need to go anywhere." Now that he'd met Robyn, he had another reason to enjoy being in Denver, but work was the best way to reason with her brothers.

Who now stared at him, jaws slack, eyes wide. Gone was their teasing humor and their previously unidentifiable expressions.

Their hope had been replaced by despair.

"We expected too much from him." Bryn sounded as disappointed in himself as in Max.

"He's back to talking about business. Same as when we first met." A flush rose on Griff's face. "We're all idiots."

"Our plan didn't work." Hedd paced in a circle, long strides sending him round and round.

"Oh, it worked." Bryn crossed to the window and leaned heavily against its frame. "Just not in our favor."

Only Griff remained facing Max, his silver eyes flashed accusingly from a face so red it rivaled his hair.

"Tell me what you hoped for?" Max demanded.

"To learn if you were man enough for our sister. You're not." Griff's fists, held rigid by his side, shook as if struggling not to strike Max for that failure.

"You're married to your business. You can't change. Not even a little." Hedd's words whipped out, quick as his strides and his wild gesturing. "But she'll change. A lot! And we'll *never*"—his arm cut the air, like an axe delivering a fatal blow—"see the real Rob again."

Max's gut coiled with dread. "She doesn't have to change."

"We know that," Griff growled.

"Unfortunately, Rob's decided differently." Bryn stood still as a statue, contemplating the city outside. "Denver's narrow-minded busybodies have made her question herself."

"Their wagging tongues speak as loudly as those who"—the scorn emanating from Griff burned Max—"say very little."

He'd said more to Robyn than anyone, but he'd clearly not said enough. "Your sister is perfect as she is."

Bryn pushed away from the window. Hedd abandoned his pacing. Both men resumed their places flanking their brother. Their reunited line of three pressed toward Max.

He didn't retreat.

"Why didn't you tell her that?" Bryn asked.

"I did."

"What else did you say?" Griff raised his index finger as if preparing to prod the answer from Max.

Max pushed his hand aside. "That I enjoy working with her. She's become my best friend."

"Lord have mercy." Hedd's spine sagged as he rubbed his brow. "This is bad."

Bryn reached around Griff and shoved Hedd's shoulder. "But not a disaster."

Hedd glared at Bryn and Max. "It is if Rob wants—"

"We Llewellyns," Bryn interrupted, "don't always get what we want. When we don't, what do we do?"

Hedd straightened like a soldier relaying an order. "We modify our plans."

The flame heating Griff's face eased. "We work with what we have."

Bryn sighed. "Dog Bone's persistence can get the job done. Work is his family, his mistress, his reason for living."

"Listen, *Big Hill.*" Max stifled the urge to jab his finger into the puffed-up chests of all three brothers while making use of his knowledge—courtesy of Robyn—of Brynmor's name in Welsh. *Bryn* meant *a hill. Brynmor* meant, even more fittingly, *a large hill.* "Can you move your lofty hulk any faster? Can any of you Llewellyns speak plainly?"

Bryn's smile held amusement and commiseration. "This month's been the busiest on record. January won't be any different. You need all hands at the ready, including Rob."

Even though he'd asked for it, the bluntness in that truth made him squirm. "She's more to me than an employee."

"Yeah, yeah." Hedd rolled his eyes. "She's your best friend."

"A good friend can save your soul," Bryn murmured.

"But not your eye," Hedd and Griff replied as one, then spun to stare at their brother with equally horrified expressions.

Bryn didn't move a muscle, but the unhinged look in his good eye raised the hair on the back of Max's neck. The calm giant often got lost in contemplation, but he'd never looked like he'd lost—everything. A beast had risen inside Bryn and devoured the soul he'd mentioned.

Hedd raised his palms and pitched his voice low and placating. "Bryn, we weren't thinking straight."

"We're idiots," Griff repeated his earlier edict. He bowed his head but kept his gaze on Bryn. "We didn't mean to say—"

"And you'll never, *ever*," Bryn snarled like a wolf reminding his pack they'd overstepped a boundary, "do so again. I refuse to waste time discussing something I can't change. Today is about Rob. Our sister has taken the lead. We do whatever it takes to help her."

"Yes, we *take care* of what he loves." Griff gestured behind Max, to the rear of the office stacked with freight awaiting transport. "His business."

"While he gets going." Hedd pointed to the door. "And brings home what we love. Our sister."

"I'd already be on my way if you'd tell me *where* Robyn went."

The three brothers exchanged glances as they said, "Noelle."

Disbelief struck Max like a rogue wave. In its wake, a cold understanding left him reeling. "This is why you questioned my resolve."

Bryn stood firm. "Saying *once* that you'd go anywhere with Rob holds little weight after saying *numerous* times you'd never return to Noelle."

Max slumped against his desk. "Why would she go there? She's never been there. She knows no one there!"

"You introduced her to your *deryn*." Griff's voice was sharp with accusation.

More waves of surprise and insight rocked him. Only his grip on his desk kept him upright. In Welsh, *deryn* meant bird. Or so Robyn had revealed after the Llewellyns had met his sister-in-law and grandpa during a Denver visit. "Birdie's been writing to Robyn."

Griff huffed. "We liked your *deryn* at first. Birdie's tiny but tough. Sweet but savvy. Then we found out she's a meddler."

"Birdie sent our *deryn* a dress and said she'd introduce Rob to women eager to teach her whatever she desires, like"—Hedd waved his hands around his head—"taming her hair and Lord knows what else."

"Honestly." Griff shot Hedd a pitying look. "Sometimes you're as scatterbrained as Max's grandfather. More than anything, Rob stressed she wanted to learn how to dance."

Max longed to learn the exact same thing. Finally, he'd have a reason to hold Robyn in his arms. "I'm going after her."

"And?" Bryn prompted.

"I'm bringing her home to Denver." Where he would convince her that they were more than friends.

"Good." Bryn looked as relieved as Max felt, now that Max had voiced his decision. "We want our sister to settle near us."

Max wanted to be even closer to her, to share a home with her. He'd build her one in Denver. He couldn't ask her to reside in his office. No more *living* only for his work. But he wasn't a master carpenter like his brother. And the winter weather would delay his start. It might take him until spring or summer before he'd be ready to court her properly. In the meantime, he could discover how interested Robyn was in marriage—especially to someone like him.

"If the right man had taken notice of her," Griff grumbled, "Rob could've married in Denver as swiftly as in Noelle."

Max's heart skipped a beat. "She mentioned marriage?"

Bryn shrugged. "We teased her about becoming a mail-order bride."

"But she said—" Hedd frowned at the ceiling as if striving to catch a wayward thought. "She didn't need a matchmaker."

"That's when she told us that your *deryn* and her married friends were going to transform her into a lady." Griff wrinkled his nose. "And that Noelle's already planning a special party that'd benefit the town and her. She hopes to see her perfect man there, and that he'll see her as a lady and propose marriage that evening."

Max reached for the calendar on his desk. "When is this party?"

"The evening of the 25th," Bryn replied.

Only four days away. He headed for the small, curtained-off section of his office where he slept so he could be near his work. The Llewellyns shadowed him like hawks.

"But don't be fooled," Bryn warned. "Despite its date, that gathering isn't a Christmas celebration."

"It's a conspiracy," Hedd jumped to add.

"Why do you say that?" Max grabbed a travel sack and searched for a clean shirt.

Without checking its condition, Griff thrust one into Max's bag. "It's an event to promote weddings."

Hedd tossed him a pair of trousers. "That's what Noelle craves most. You can't even invest in its silver mine if you aren't married."

The Llewellyns threw him items to pack as quickly as they threw him advice.

"Don't trust anyone, including your sister-in-law."

"And your brother."

"And your grandfather. He might be the worst."

"Couldn't stop pestering us about when we'd all get hitched."

"The whole town will be wanting Rob to marry and stay in Noelle."

"You gotta convince her to leave before the 25th."

Max scrubbed his hand over his beard, trying to think how he'd accomplish that. Instead, his thoughts went to how Robyn's eyes lit up whenever she called him Red Beard, a name her brothers refused to repeat since they believed his blond hair overshadowed any red in his beard.

"Hurry up." Hedd hurled Max's shaving brush and soap at him. "You can spruce up later. After you get to Noelle."

Bryn handed Max his razor before Hedd could lob it at him as well. "Be prepared to change to compete with those infamous Noelle bachelors, but keep insisting Rob does *not* have to change. Tell her she's needed in Denver. Right now. We've lots of work and we can't handle it all ourselves."

At least that was the truth. He wouldn't have to lie. "But what if...?" Max trailed off, struggling with the alternative.

"She won't leave Noelle?" Griff folded his arms decisively. "Then you need to sabotage her transformation."

"Get her involved in your family's business," Hedd ordered. "Fabricate work if need be. Don't give Rob time to change."

"But if she truly wants to be different," Max said, "she'll find a way." And if they all wanted the best for Robyn, shouldn't they let her?

"Our Rob's resourceful." Bryn's voice vibrated with pride and apprehension.

Max dug his best suit, heck his only suit, out from the bottom of a trunk. He prayed he wouldn't have to don it for a party.

"But you're tenacious." Hedd snatched the garment from his hands and thrust it into the bag.

Griff pushed him toward the door. "You're Dog Bone. Once you've sunk your teeth into a task, you'll do everything in your power to complete it."

"And above all, you're Rob's best friend." Bryn's voice, deep and final as a judge's verdict, played havoc with Max's hope that he could be more than that. "So, do what's best for her and us. Catch the next train to Noelle and bring our sister home. If you fail, everything changes. We'll have to join Rob in Noelle and leave you in Denver to run your beloved business. Alone."

CHAPTER 2

Noelle, Colorado
Later that day and...
Four days until Christmas and the party

*D*resses were menaces. The dratted skirt caught on the saddle and nearly upended Robyn as she dismounted from Caradoc. She landed with a curse and a flurry of fabric. The usually unrufflable Clydesdale snorted, sharing her surprise. Her Noelle endeavor suddenly loomed a thousand times larger than her usual jaunts in Denver hauling Peregrine freight.

She'd never regret taking the old road to Noelle rather than the train. She'd always wanted to experience the iconic trail that Max had hauled freight up and down so many times in the past.

But perhaps she should've waited to don her new attire until *after* arriving in Noelle. Her eagerness to begin her transformation as soon as possible might not have been wise.

She'd misjudged a dress' unique challenges. Wearing a skirt was hard work. Why did women consent to do it?

In trousers, she could've sprung from Caradoc's back in one smooth leap. No frustration. No fuss. No flash of petticoats, like a flag announcing her arrival. Her unladylike dismount brought stares, whistles, and even catcalls from the men on the street between the train depot and Noelle's Peregrines' Post and Freight office.

Her expletive about foul-smelling goats shocked them into silence. Not very ladylike either, but effective. Would apologizing for her lack of grace have been the correct response?

She'd have to ask Noelle's married ladies.

Giving the men a final glare, she spun on her heel to tie Caradoc's reins to Peregrines' hitching rail.

Before she could, the office door opened, and Birdie stepped out and enveloped her in a hug. "*Voilà*, you're here! And how delighted we are to finally see you in Noelle."

Trying not to squirm like a gangly gosling under a mother's wing, Robyn patted Birdie's shoulder. Coming from a family of brothers who seldom hugged, she often wondered how Birdie—who'd grown up with brothers whose dishonorable deeds had forced her to assume a false name and live a life of hiding until she came to Noelle—had become so open with her emotions.

When a man who resembled Max—except with wilder hair, a blonder beard, and lighter eyes—appeared, she understood. Birdie released Robyn and stepped into the circle of her husband's arms. She flew to him like a bird to a nest.

Love had changed her.

It had changed Robyn as well, but only her heart. Noelle

and its women were her best hope for changing all of her. Then she might win her own love.

Jack draped a long coat around Birdie and drew her close to his side. "Welcome to Noelle," he said when he finally dragged his attention away from his wife and smiled at Robyn. "Birdie and Grandpa haven't stopped talking about you since their first Denver visit."

"Hallelujah!" Grandpa Gus burst out of the office, straightening his flat cap and smoothing his carrot-colored hair as if preparing to greet a princess. "My favorite Llewellyn has arrived." He reached for Caradoc's reins. "Let me take the Clyde 'round back."

In one smooth move, Birdie linked arms with Gus, stopping the old man's advance, while Jack said, "I'll settle the horse in the barn while you three go inside and get reacquainted."

Even though she knew the couple collaborated to reduce Gus' workload, Robyn bristled at being coddled as well. It reminded her too much of her brothers' meddling.

She held her hand behind her back with the reins out of reach. "I'll take Caradoc. Tending him is my most important job." And she also wanted a peek at the marvelous mules Max had mentioned. She was eager to learn everything about Noelle and its freight business.

"Ours too," Jack said with conviction. "He's part of our family."

"But when he lived with us, he was only the Clyde." Gus stroked Caradoc's wide white blaze and the horse nickered softly. "Yes, you remember. I helped raise you before you became entirely Max's horse. Now we reunite bearing fancy new names. Mine's *Grand-père*."

"Caradoc sounds Welsh." Birdie, who'd been born in Quebec and was fluent in French, had taken a keen interest in the Llewellyns' penchant for nicknames and their translations. "What does it mean?"

Robyn's cheeks grew warm. Many months ago, she'd whispered the word while working beside Max. He also asked what it meant. She'd lied and said it was her name for his horse. Today, she busied herself loosening Caradoc's cinch and patting his mahogany coat—the color warm and rich as Max's eyes. "Caradoc means dearly loved."

"Lucky horse," Gus replied, "to be so treasured by you 'n my grandson."

"Our connection may be temporary." The realization that her words applied to not only Caradoc but Max made her frown. "I only have him on loan."

She couldn't tell Gus or Jack—or even Birdie—the whole truth. She couldn't tell Max either. Loving him jeopardized everything she'd gained. The one man willing to employ her to drive a wagon had become her best friend. He was also the only boss her brothers had ever enjoyed working with. They teased Max terribly; their version of giving a hug.

And her?

She couldn't stop wanting Max to see her as more than a friend.

She needed to proceed carefully but quickly, before another woman snared his attention. Mail-order bride mania gripped the state. Maybe even the entire country.

Men wanted women who were...well, women. Every story Birdie had shared about the brides of Noelle had shown her that. Those women all wore dresses. She didn't know what else they did, but she was determined to find out.

When Birdie mentioned the bride—who'd married the diner owner—was a dancer, Robyn's plan had grown wings.

If she knew the ways of a lady and if Josefina Villanueva could teach her to waltz in a dress, she could dance at a party and impress Max. *If* he returned to Noelle.

"The snow's stopped, but it's still cold out here," Jack said, as if that were news. His brow furrowed as he contemplated Birdie. "You and Grandpa should go inside while Miss Llewellyn and I stow Caradoc."

Gus' smile became a scowl. "You keep runnin' the conversation back to the Clyde. I've forgotten something again, haven't I?" His bushy brows shot up as his gaze pinned Robyn. "You have Max's horse, 'n that boy would never let him go easily."

She hoped that was the case. Caradoc's departure might provide incentive for Max to come to Noelle.

"Have you stolen him?" Gus' eyes widened with a puzzled curiosity.

"*Grand-père*," Birdie said with a laugh. "Robyn said she has Max's horse on loan."

"Did she now?" Gus tapped his chin. "That fits with him sayin' he spent more time organizing freight this summer than hauling it." He thrust his finger in the air like he'd found the answer. "The Clyde needed a new partner. Max chose you 'n the Clyde agreed." Gus went back to tapping his chin. "Or maybe it was the other way 'round?"

Jack held Birdie even closer as he stared at the road leading to Denver. "Besides one wagon, the Clyde was all Max took when he left us."

"You haven't lost him forever," Birdie said gently. "He'll return when he's ready."

Jack sighed, sounding a lot like Brynmor fighting a private battle while unwilling to burden others. "And if my brother's never ready?"

A twinge of guilt pierced Robyn. She wanted Max in

Denver with her and her brothers, but Max's family wanted him in Noelle. And Max wanted one thing. "He's determined to make his Denver office a success."

Jack snorted. "I've no doubt he's already accomplished that. Max's resolve is legendary." His shoulders sagged. "Now he's committed to staying away."

"Or maybe he's just busy," Birdie said. "Denver moves at a bustling pace. Faster than I remember from my days running a dress shop there."

Jack shifted his weight to his good leg. "Denver can't be busier than Noelle. And in this town, I have both freight and carpentry to deal with. Max only has the freight."

"Brotherly admiration and rivalry. What a pair you are." Birdie rolled her eyes, then winked at Robyn. "And you and Max, too." Her gaze narrowed with determination. "We only change when *we* are ready. Are *you* ready to visit the dancing lady?"

"Birdie, you shouldn't—" Jack flinched when his wife withdrew from his embrace. "Consider the options. It's late in the day, and our guest has had a long journey." He gave Robyn a pleading look. "You both should— You both *could* recuperate inside the office before venturing into town."

"I'm not tired." Birdie's gaze remained on Robyn. "And you?"

"Too excited to be tired." *And nervous.* "I've so much to learn." *And I only have four days.*

"I'm fit as a fiddle," Gus proclaimed. "And rarin' to go, too. I'll dance with every gal in town."

"Miss Llew— *Robyn*," Jack said her name on the weariest sigh she'd ever heard. "We've only met, but I must beg your assistance." He gestured to Gus and Birdie. "As you can see, I'm outnumbered, but have you also seen that I'm about to become a father?"

Robyn's gaze plummeted to Birdie's rounded belly, peaking through the opening of the coat Jack had so diligently draped over his wife's shoulders.

She blinked in disbelief. How could she be so dense? Was she so consumed by her own worries that she couldn't see the obvious?

"Surprise," Birdie said with a half shrug and a huge smile.

"The best ever!" She clapped her hands. "You must be excited and—" She froze when she saw Jack's still pleading expression.

He and Birdie, even if she wasn't showing it, had to be more nervous than Robyn could ever be. At least until she was married and with child and— She was getting ahead of herself. She had four days to change Max's view of her. But in those days, she must also help his family, who'd become her friends and who might one day, if she was lucky, be her family as well.

She pressed her palm to her heart and said as solemnly as she could, "You have my full support."

"Thank you." Jack's deep voice rumbled with relief.

She turned to his grandfather. "Gus, will you—?"

"No," the old-timer grumbled with a vigorous shake of his head. "I ain't doing nothin' unless you call me Grandpa or—"

"*Bon-papa*," Robyn interrupted because she liked the French translations better than the Welsh, but she didn't want to intrude on Birdie's special name for Gus. She also didn't want to keep all three Peregrines standing in the cold any longer. "Will you show me the barn?"

Jack's groan made her add, "Will you also stay with me until we return to your office? I'm not one to get lost, not after hauling freight around a city's rabbit warren of streets, but..." She flashed the smile she used to cajole her brothers. "I do like company."

"And I'd be delighted to be yer escort, pretty lady." Halfway to the barn, Gus glanced behind him, then leaned closer to her and whispered, "Good. We ain't being followed. They often do that. Got noses like bloodhounds, they do."

His comparison made her inhale deeply. Noelle's crisp mountain air invigorated her mood. A small town like this had to be different from Denver in more ways than she could imagine. Anticipation quickened her pace. The memory of not paying attention to the people closest to her made her slow her steps to match Gus'. Which wasn't a hardship.

For his age, he was fleet of foot, if not always of mind.

A fierce affection for him, and the family who adored him to the point of smothering him, welled up inside Robyn. The extent of her feelings bewildered her until she remembered what Max had told her.

His grandfather had been involved in Max and Jack's lives longer than their father had. Not by choice, but by circumstance. The War Between the States had torn the middle out of their family. The Peregrines had lost a father and a son to a wagon accident that'd rattle even the most hardened of freighters.

Max had a steely determination, but his heart wasn't cold or closed. He'd given her a job without a lecture about a woman's inability to do the work. He hadn't ended her employment, or even reduced her load, after the days when freight runs got challenging, as they sooner or later did.

He'd accepted her as she was.

She'd admired him for that. She still did, but she couldn't stop craving more. Which jeopardized their friendship and her growing connection to his grandfather. "I wish we were already family."

"Already?" The knowing glint in Gus' golden eyes made her duck her head.

"I know," she mumbled. "I'm rushing things."

"In that, yer like yer brother, Heddwyn."

"I hope I'm like Brynmor and Griffin, too."

"You are. None of you can stop hoping fer a better future, but you need to be careful what you wish fer." He heaved a sigh. "If a Peregrine has to, they can make it darned difficult for a person to have any fun. Now it's my turn."

Noelle's crisp air suddenly felt frigid. "Your turn for what?"

"To be the voice of reason. The bearer of bad news. The fly in yer honey." He snorted a laugh. "Or is it ointment? Can't remember. But you gotta remember—" He shook his finger at her. "Don't shoot me. I'm only the messenger."

His flurry of words made her thoughts spin. She planted her feet in the snow and demanded, "What are you talking about?"

"Max, of course. Which is a topic best discussed in private." Gus opened the barn door and gestured for her to lead Caradoc inside.

Her eagerness to learn anything about Max made her follow his directions without question. The barn's dark interior contrasted starkly with the snowy mountain outside, where nature's glory had been broken by only three manmade structures: a town, a railroad track, and a telegraph line.

Her heart skipped a beat.

While she'd been riding away from her brothers, knowing she'd be spending her first Christmas without them, had they sent a telegram to Noelle? What if something happened to them or Max while she was gone?

She seized Gus' arm. "Has someone—?" *Died*. She couldn't say the word. She pressed her lips tight and clutched Gus' arm even tighter. "Been hurt?"

"What? No! Tarnation, girl." He lit a lantern and used its glow to inspect her face. "Yer skin is as white as a snowsquall, 'n yer eyes are as big as—"

"Enough about me." She yanked his sleeve impatiently. "What's your message?"

"The Clyde needs tending to." When she opened her mouth to argue, he held up his hand. "We can talk while we work."

"Fine." She undid Caradoc's cinch, a familiar task that allowed her to keep her gaze on Gus as he crossed to a row of stabled mules. The ones she'd been so eager to see. She spared them barely a glance before studying Gus again.

What was his message? Why wouldn't he tell her? Was he disappointed, or angry, or—?

Gus cleared his throat gruffly as he pulled a pitchfork from a haystack. "I know why you've come to Noelle, but you'd best watch yer step. You need to protect yerself."

"Learning how to dance isn't dangerous." She grasped the horn, sitting high on Caradoc's back, and slid the saddle toward her.

Gus pitched hay into a corner of an empty stall. "Yer risk ain't in waltzing, but in being sweet on my grandson."

His sudden directness made her hold on the saddle slip. The leather seat struck her chest like a giant slap in the face. She was lucky it hadn't rotated as it fell. The horn would've knocked the breath out of her completely.

She muttered a string of curses as she balanced the

saddle on her hip and used her free hand to rub the sting from her chest. "Who told you that?"

Enticed by his dinner, Caradoc trotted into the open stall. Gus removed his bridle so he could eat unfettered, then commenced brushing, which made the horse snuffle and sigh happily between mouthfuls of hay.

"Who said I'm—?" She waved her hand in the air, searching for the words to express her feelings for Max.

"Hopelessly in love with the wrong man?"

"Yes. No!" She dropped the saddle and set her hands on her hips. "Why would you call Max that? He's the right man. The only one for me. And you haven't answered my question. Who told you?"

"That yer besotted? Smitten? Hooked like a fish? Fallen head over heels? Or is it heels over head? Or arse over—?"

"All right. I'm all of that. Now tell me *who* told you."

"You did."

Her mouth fell open like the fish Gus had compared her to. Except she wasn't hooked onto anything now. She was floundering. "I never said a word."

"Didn't have to. It's how you look at him. How yer voice changes when you talk about him."

"Does Max know?" *Please don't say you've told him! I need to change first. I need time to make him see me as more than a friend.*

"Not likely. Not with his thoughts always on work. He's the same as Jack was before marrying Birdie. Now even their honeymoon bliss is gone. Impending fatherhood has Jack back to fretting 'n working more hours than not. I'm worried again."

"I'm sorry to hear that. I wish I could help, but I can't. Not with Jack's workload, at least. I have my own work in Denver."

"But if you stay there—working all day, every day as hard as Max 'n probably yer brothers too, you won't marry. None of you will. You'll grow old waiting fer Max to take notice of you."

She released an indignant breath as she picked up Caradoc's saddle and set it on the rack holding the wagon harnesses. "I'm not waiting any longer. I'm making changes."

"But are they the right kind?" Gus tapped his chest. "I know matchmakers in Noelle who, I wager, can find you a husband who'll accept you as you are."

"I don't want those men! I want Max. And those husbands you mention, here in Noelle or anywhere else, don't exist. No man wants a wife who wears trousers."

"How do you know?" Gus asked.

"I know what I've seen. Men pay attention to women who wear—" She groaned when her gaze found her skirt covered in bits of straw. "No one wants this," she grumbled as she pointed at the disorder that had sprung out of nowhere to mar her transformation.

"Don't be so certain. I'd love to have you, *exactly as you are*, as my granddaughter."

Tears pricked her eyes. When Gus held out his hand, she hesitated for only a heartbeat before she ran to grab it.

She wanted to stay in Noelle with him, but she couldn't without Max by her side. "Help me change Max."

"No."

She jerked away from him in disbelief. "Why not?"

"Because he's happy where he is. Listen, I'd gladly help you *show* my grandson what he's missing if he were here." His voice grew thick with emotion. "Unfortunately, Max ain't comin' home fer Christmas. Nor will he, like Birdie hopes, be visiting Noelle any time after that. He doesn't need you 'n me. Not like Jack 'n Birdie do."

The lump in her throat made it hard to speak. "But I need him."

"You need new opportunities before you'll know that fer sure. You could take the reins here in Noelle. Then Jack could stay in his carpentry shop or whatever building he's constructing in town. Heck, he could even do an occasional stint at the office if need be."

She couldn't help but scowl like a petulant child about to be denied her favorite toy. "I'm happiest driving wagons."

"If you find the right partner, he could do the office work."

"Max does that."

"He also enjoys being a bachelor more than being a family man."

He might change. But Gus was right. It wasn't right to push Max to change if he was happy as he was now.

A frown pinched Gus' brow. "What did my grandson say about yer comin' to Noelle?"

"I didn't tell him. My brothers said they'd inform him. I hoped they might inspire him to follow me."

Gus shrugged. "Even if they did, they can't inspire him to complete such a journey. He'll turn back."

"What makes you so certain?"

"Yer story 'bout him givin' you the Clyde. Was a time, not long ago, when all Max wanted was to get on the road with that horse. Now he's found something he likes better. Staying put in a bustling city where he's king of his castle. Noelle ain't big enough for Max."

"But the town's growing," she protested, hoping that might somehow entice Max to come to Noelle.

"Not fast enough fer some. And that shouldn't concern you if yer makin' yer decisions for yerself 'n not for my grandson—who you won't see dancing at a party in Noelle this Christmas."

CHAPTER 3

*W*ith Jack and Birdie leading the way, and Gus by her side, Robyn trudged down Noelle's main street toward her future. Whatever it might be. The town that Birdie had described so passionately in her letters failed to revive her enthusiasm. Without the prospect of Max joining her in Noelle, how could it?

She peered behind her, scanning the junction where the street turned toward Denver, hoping to glimpse a man she now had to accept she wouldn't see any time soon. For the reasons Gus had explained, plus one more.

As Brynmor often warned, *only the daft, the desperate, or the devil traveled the wilderness after dusk.* Which was coming quickly. Twilight darkened the snowdrifts under the frost-tipped evergreens that now appeared black.

When she faced forward again, she found Jack's worried gaze on Birdie, and Birdie's equally concerned gaze on her.

Too much looking back. She squared her shoulders and studied the nearest structure. "The Golden Nugget Saloon looks splendid. Is that one of the renovations you mentioned?"

"*Oui.* Both Jack and Gus," Birdie said proudly, "had a hand in that, and several new builds. Wait till you see Elwood Hunter's bookstore at the end of the street. It's not far. We could go there now."

"You'll see everything better when the sun's up and it's warmer and..." Jack trailed off as Birdie's chin raised mulishly.

Robyn scrambled for a way to turn the conversation. "Sheridan's Hardware looks closed for the evening. I imagine the bookstore is the same. Since I'm keen to see interiors and exteriors, let's delay any town tour until the morning."

A relieved smile lightened Jack's countenance until Gus said, "Cobb's Penn is also closed, but you can still see Daphne's hats in their window."

"This is something I can't wait to show you!" Birdie grabbed her hand and tugged her off the street and onto the walkway outside the general store.

Birdie made the leap in one nimble step. Robyn did not. Her toe caught on the hem of her skirt. She stumbled like a drunk and swore just as incoherently as one. Only Birdie's steadying hand kept her upright, while Jack and Gus, bless them, made no comment on her lack of grace.

Jack positioned himself close to Birdie so she wouldn't have to release Robyn's hand. He held out his arm to his wife. Birdie snuggled close to her husband's side and gazed up at him with so much love that Robyn's chest grew tight with envy.

"This is my favorite spot," Birdie murmured.

Jack's huff sounded oddly amused. "I'll admit," he drawled, "that Cobb's Penn has better windows than Peregrines' Post, but surely that's not enough to garner such favoritism?"

Birdie snorted an unladylike laugh, but her voice was as pleasant as a Sunday prayer when she murmured, "*Charmant bourreau des coeurs.*"

Gus grinned as he waggled his finger at his grandson. "She knows you too well, Sunny Boy."

But Robyn did not. "What am I missing?"

"That yer family ain't the only ones fond of names. *Sunny Boy,*" Gus said with a distant look in his eyes, "was what I called Jack when he was young 'n radiated happiness." He frowned. "Before the war 'n what came afterward."

"And *charmant bourreau des coeurs*?" Robyn asked, hoping to distract the Peregrines from those difficult times.

"Means charming heartbreaker," Birdie replied quickly, probably eager to divert their thoughts as well. "My name for Jack and his teasing when he knows all too well that *where* I am is not what I love best, but *who* I'm with—my husband, my *grand-père,* and our good friend." Her gaze held Robyn's. "Remember when I wrote to you that Daphne and I were collaborating on ensembles?"

"Daphne's hats and your dresses. A head to hem pairing."

Birdie's eyes widened. "You quote my exact words."

Robyn shrugged, embarrassed to reveal how many times she'd read Birdie's letters.

"*Zut de zut!*" Birdie released Robyn's hand and tapped herself soundly on the temple. "What a dolt I am. I should have sent one of Daphne's bonnets with your dress. First thing tomorrow, we shall obtain you a new *chapeau.*"

Robyn's hand flew to her knitted wool cap. Replacing her trousers was one thing, but giving up her hat?

Birdie gestured to the finery in the window. "Which one do you like best?"

All of them, and none of them. They were beautiful, but...

"I like my cap best. It's warm, and even though it's plain in color, it's exquisitely soft, and was made in a way that is precious to my heart." Robyn knew she was rambling, but she couldn't stop. "The wool came from sheep farmers who'd recently emigrated from Spain."

"Let me guess," Gus said. "They couldn't afford to pay Max, so the wool was their gift to him? And your cap became Max's gift to you?"

"Not only me. Last Christmas, he also made caps for each of my brothers."

Jack stared at her as if bewildered. "My brother knitted hats for all of you?"

"Of course, he did," Robyn said, perturbed. "Why should that surprise you?"

"Because I thought Max was too busy for knitting. I also assumed he'd grown tired of folks ribbing him whenever they saw him knitting, which he often did in our office. He only stopped a week before he left Noelle." Jack's expression turned as perturbed as she'd felt prior to his explanation. "Did your brothers make fun of him too?"

"*Never*. My brothers may also be *charmants bourreaux*, but they'd never tease Max about the caps he made for us. Not after he took the time to make them look like the one Bryn inherited from our father."

Birdie took hold of her hand again and squeezed it reassuringly. "Your brothers said he died before you were born, and your mother soon afterward. I'm sorry you didn't get to know them."

"Bryn tells so many stories that it feels like I do know them. He says Papa told him his cap was made in our ancestors' home in Monmouth. Since the wool began coming apart, Bryn has kept the hat in his pocket and won't let anyone mend it. Says every stitch, even the unraveled ones, tells us something about who we are and where we came from; the same as words in a journal."

Gus pressed closer to Cobb's Penn's window. "Do you see any needles inside? I want to learn how to knit."

Jack cleared his throat. "Grandpa, you've already learned how."

"I have not." Gus stiffened. "What have I forgotten now?"

"Remember when we came home after the war?" Jack asked.

"You took up carpentry 'n Max started knitting."

"And who taught Max?"

"Yer gran did." Tears glistened in Gus' eyes. "Then she tried to teach me."

"But you were always better at leather tooling. And last year you did some mighty fine wood whittling."

Gus swiped his hand across his eyes and straightened his back. "And maybe, this year, I'll do some *mighty fine* knitting. I'll make caps fer everyone, myself included."

"But would you wear it?" Robyn wondered if she'd wear anything other than Max's cap.

When Gus opened his mouth to argue, she said, "You enjoy your flat cap too much. And I love my wool cap and..." She contemplated Daphne's hats, so different from what she wore. "Do women wear hats like mine?"

"Hmm, I can't rightly say." Gus tapped his chin, the same as he'd done outside Peregrines' Post when he'd pondered her stealing Max's horse. "I should focus on something everyone wears."

"Or perhaps not wears but simply *needs*?" Jack asked. "Like food and a fire to warm themselves? Like we'll find at Nacho's?"

She'd forgotten about the diner. When she pivoted to face it, her companions turned with her, finally in accord.

"Time to meet the dancing lady," Birdie said.

Robyn had forgotten about that as well. Did she need to learn to dance if Max wouldn't be at Noelle's Christmas party? Should she just go home?

"I'm eager for everyone to meet you." Birdie cut a diagonal course across the street that'd allow them to reach the diner in the least number of steps.

"I can't stay long." Her words spilled out without thought and warning.

All three Peregrines slowed their pace. The air vibrated with unasked questions.

"But I said I'd stay for Christmas, and I will." And if she didn't fill her time with dancing and planning a new future, what should she do? The diner's sign caught her attention. *Nacho's Tacos.* An intriguing name and maybe a delicious distraction. "I've never had tacos. Are they good?"

"You might never find out," Gus grumbled. "We'll be lucky if our meal ain't interrupted nonstop."

"By?"

Gus waved his arms in the air. "Talk of work: to be done, that ain't been done, or not done fast enough. The town's in a flutter from all the railroad politics 'n an unquenchable thirst fer progress. Christmas should be a time to slow down 'n count yer blessings. But oh no, everyone wants their deliveries 'n dreams handed to them immediately. They can't wait any longer."

They sounded like she'd felt. Spending her time learning something as frivolous as dancing now seemed both selfish and pointless. Dancing with a partner who wasn't Max wouldn't make her happy, but if she helped the Peregrines with their work, she could make them happy, and maybe a whole lot of other folks in Noelle as well.

Folks she'd read about in letters and would soon meet.

She watched Birdie lift her skirt enough to allow her to gracefully step onto the boardwalk outside Nacho's. She mimicked the action and couldn't help but grin when she didn't trip.

Maybe dresses weren't so bad after all.

Jack held open Nacho's front door for them to enter. As he did, a gust of wind hit Robyn's legs and twisted her skirt around her ankles. She kicked at the hem to straighten it. When it resisted, her curse was strong and clear. A hard yank finally set her to order and allowed her to stand tall and view her surroundings.

Every man in the room gaped at her. She searched for a woman's face. For Josefina or Daphne or... Who else had Birdie written about? The woman who ran the general store across the street. What was her name? Avis! Yes, Avis probably sold many helpful products that'd be a mystery to most.

Robyn ran her hand over her long braid. What might Avis recommend for subduing curly hair, currently half-tamed in a practical plait?

Jack led their party to an empty table.

Gus stayed close to her and whispered, "Good job on making yer entrance memorable. I count ten bachelors still staring at you. One of them could be yer future husband."

An unbearable ache rose in her chest as she imagined Max not filling that role and them no longer working together. The sight of Birdie gathering her skirt to sit provided a welcome distraction. She concentrated on copying her movements.

"Which man should we talk to first?" Gus asked.

"None of them," she muttered as she claimed her seat without a hitch.

"But—"

She crossed her ankles demurely and her arms stubbornly. "*First*, I want to meet Josefina."

"And here I am."

Robyn's arms dropped to her sides as she gaped at the woman in front of her. Birdie's description failed to prepare her for the vitality the dancing lady exuded.

"And I have my pot of chocolate," Josefina declared with a smile as she raised a kettle that traditionally would've held coffee. "Shall I pour you a round?"

When everyone agreed and the task was completed, Josefina offered her hand to Robyn.

She froze. She wasn't comfortable shaking hands or hugging people or— If she didn't change this, how could she expect to change anything else? She seized Josefina's hand and shook it so heartily that she amazed herself.

"I'm also happy to finally meet you." A teasing glint sparked in Josefina's eyes as she glanced at Birdie. "A little bird has pestered my ears continually about you."

Birdie laughed. "And I intend to pester you more tonight."

"But first," Jack rushed to say, "could we order food? Birdie needs— We all need some nourishment."

"Sure. What will you have?" Josefina asked.

"A...taco?" Robyn replied uncertainly.

"I'll have the same," Gus said.

"And us as well." Birdie patted Jack's hand. "I'm ready to eat."

Jack sighed with relief, then chuckled when Birdie added, "A lot."

As Josefina departed, Robyn noticed the men at the surrounding tables still stared at her. She chose to ignore them by focusing on her drink. The delicious chocolate warmed and relaxed her. She hoped the taco was as good and that she could savor it without speaking to any bachelors, or without the Peregrines being hounded about freight jobs.

Blessedly, only the buzz of whispered conversations disturbed the room.

When Josefina returned with a tall, dark-haired man who expertly balanced their plates while exchanging adoring smiles with Josefina, Robyn knew he must be Nacho Villanueva.

When the last plate was set on the table, a hesitant voice said, "Could I have some of that chocolate, Mrs. Villanueva?"

A "me too" chorus came from the surrounding tables.

"But first," said the man who'd made the initial request, "make sure that lovely lady gets her cup refilled."

Robyn's gaze swept the room, eager to find the lady he meant. Her jaw dropped when she found him pointing at her. Her amazement turned to annoyance when she also found his gaze on her figure rather than her face.

She was more than what she wore!

Max looked her in the eye when he spoke to her and not *about* her. He also wasn't here. A fierce longing to see him again overshadowed her delight in being with the Peregrines and the Villanuevas.

Fully committed to replacing dancing—and all types of socializing—with working, Robyn faced Josefina, who was filling her cup. "Mrs. Villanueva, for the duration of my stay in Noelle—"

"Please call me Josefina or even Fina."

"Fina, about my lessons—"

A chill breeze ruffled her skirt as the diner door banged open. A group of dusty miners burst into the room, hollering good-naturedly for their dinner orders.

"Hold that thought," Fina called over her shoulder as she followed her husband back to their kitchen. "I'll return as soon as I can."

Robyn ground her teeth in frustration. Her trip to Noelle wasn't going as she'd hoped. Nor were her attempts to regain control of her venture. Maybe her comfortable, but not totally fulfilling routine in Denver wasn't so bad. At least there, she'd held the reins and knew her destination.

"Miss?" The query, hesitant but hopeful, came from her left.

She stared at her cup and prayed the man was talking to Birdie, which was ridiculous because Birdie was a Mrs.

"Here it comes," Gus whispered in her ear. "Yer first proposal."

Surely a man wouldn't ask to wed a woman he hadn't even conversed with. Her certainty wavered when she remembered most of Noelle's mail-order marriages had started that way. But hadn't those couples formed a bond, no matter how small, through letters prior to their meeting?

She longed to feel that connection as well.

"Miss," the man repeated with a dogged determination that reminded her of Max.

Max had never ignored a challenge, and neither should she.

She turned to face her chatty neighbor head on. "What do you want?"

He gulped and mumbled, "Me and my friends..." He gestured to the men at his table. "We were hoping you might...clear up a question we have."

"About marriage?" Gus asked eagerly.

"In...a way, yeah." The man's voice gained volume. "It's about wives."

"See!" Gus boasted. "I was right."

"Fine." She stomped her foot. "Let's get this over with. Ask and I will answer." A resounding *no!*

Oblivious to her ire, the man smiled. "Are you related to Seamus' wife or to Doc Deane's?"

Confusion held her tongue-tied. She'd reread Birdie's letters about the women of Noelle until she felt like she'd known them all her life. But why would this man believe she was related to two strangers who'd come to Noelle separately but for similar marriage-minded reasons? She couldn't have heard him correctly. "Do you mean Norah and Cara?"

He nodded as vigorously as the men seated around them. They all stared at her expectantly. "Yes, the redheads."

Irritation made Robyn bristle. "They have names, you know. A woman isn't just somebody's wife or a hair color."

The man dropped his gaze along with his voice. "Meant no offense. Sorry."

She felt like she'd kicked the stuffing out of a daft but still brave scarecrow. "Apology accepted. Now, to answer your question. No, I have not had the pleasure of meeting *Norah* or *Cara,* let alone the gift of being their kinfolk."

"But you know their names, and you have red hair like theirs and—"

"Hair!" Robyn seized her braid; certain she now had the answer to one of her questions.

The man cringed. "Sorry again to speak of—" He waved at her hair. "Is it a forbidden subject?"

"I hope not." She pivoted on her seat to face Birdie. "Do you think Norah or Cara could offer advice for changing my hair?" Her shoulders drooped. Further transformations were pointless if Max wasn't near to bear witness.

"Why'd you want to do that?" her chatty neighbor asked. "You got pretty hair."

"See?" Gus' elbow poked her side and made her sit straighter. "Yer perfect as you are."

"Yeah," said the man who'd asked about her relations. "You should be proud to be Irish."

His advice turned her spine as stiff as a wagon seat with no springs. "I most certainly am not!"

Again, the men blinked in surprise.

"I'm proud to be *Welsh*," she clarified.

"Ah," he said, as if he now knew everything about her. "You come from mining folk."

"No, my family and I are teamsters."

"You're a...?" Too perplexed to even complete his sentence, the man scratched his head.

"A wagon driver. Yes."

"Well, ain't that something." His tone left her perplexed again.

"Something suddenly *less perfect?*" she demanded.

He shrugged. "Something different. Thought most Welsh workers found their calling down a mineshaft."

One of his friends cut in. "You mentioned family. Is your husband a mule skinner too?"

A surge of stubborn resistance made her answer only part of his question. "We don't always drive mules. We have horses too."

Gus' fingers drummed the table. "She forgot to mention she ain't married."

The men's eyes lit up as they leaned toward her.

She met their stares without blinking and said as ominously as she could, "But I have three extremely large brothers."

That news brought wariness to their interest.

"Who live in Denver." Gus slapped the table hard. "Gentlemen, enough dillydallyin'. Let me introduce you to Miss

Robyn Llewellyn, who will be spending Christmas with us in Noelle. So, save a dance for her at the party 'n— Ouch!" Gus scowled at her. "Why'd you step on my toe?"

Robyn sprang to her feet, planted her hands on her hips, and muttered, "Because, *Bon-papa*, you know there is only one man I wish to dance with."

"And he ain't here. So, save yer crossness for when you see him."

A second bang of the door and a flurry of chill winter air heralded the arrival of another diner. In the doorway stood a tall, fair-haired man with a red beard. Not bright red, but still red. A warm shade of cinnamon that had become her favorite.

Her heart skipped a beat. Max had come to Noelle.

"What—?" Gus' voice cracked, then grew thick with emotion. "What did I say? Always knew he'd come back." He cleared his throat and shouted, "Welcome home, Maximilian Boy!"

Gus' reversal of opinion made her groan, but not for long. She shared his elation to see Max.

Her heart raced with excitement as she tried to smooth her skirt and her hair. The skirt obeyed. The strands escaping her braid did not. Too curly, too wild, too unladylike!

She must arrange to talk to the redheads, Norah and Cara, after all. And speak to Avis about hair taming products. And while she was at Avis' store, purchase one of Daphne's hats. And, above all else, learn how to dance from Fina.

Against the odds, Max had come to Noelle. She must hold her faith that whatever happened next, whatever Max did or didn't do, her plan to see how Noelle might change them both was in motion. She couldn't turn back.

CHAPTER 4

*M*ax stood, astounded. Not by how much Noelle had changed, but by how little he had. Hovering inside Nacho's front door with so many unenthused faces staring at him, he still felt like an outsider, a fraud, a square post in a round hole. Every success he'd earned since leaving Noelle seemed insignificant or, even worse, like none of it had happened.

He considered turning tail and heading back to Denver. As fast as he could. Then Grandpa shouted his name, and he saw him, Jack, Birdie, and—

He shook his head in disbelief.

Was that Robyn? Wearing a dress? Surrounded by a roomful of men? Men who dismissed him and pinned their gazes on her. With too much enthusiasm.

He made a beeline for her. His brother leapt from his seat and intercepted him. Max held out his hand for a welcoming handshake, but Jack yanked him in for a fierce hug.

"You're back." Jack squeezed him even tighter.

"And you're cracking my ribs."

The instant Jack released him, Gus hugged him just as intensely. Birdie did as well. When he was finally free, he still struggled to breathe. Their exuberant greeting overwhelmed him.

He coughed and said, "It's good to be here with you." He meant it even more when he saw Robyn smiling at him.

"And what brings you here, Red Beard?" The familiar spark in her eyes when she said her special name for him made it even harder to draw in air. Unexpectedly, her eyes darkened and her voice wavered as she said, "I hope...everything is well in Denver."

"Your brothers are good." As good as he could imagine them ever being. "I'm here for you." He forgot to breathe entirely when her eyes shone brighter than he'd ever seen. "You're needed in Denver, Red Bird."

"Red Bird?" a nearby diner repeated like a squawky parrot. "Ain't that the name of the Denver stage?"

A fork clattered on a plate. "It's bad luck to name a stagecoach after a woman."

"Yer thinking of ships."

"Naming 'em after women or having women aboard 'em?"

"Probably both."

The men's absurd conversation riled his temper. So did the fact that when he spared them a glance, he found them still staring ardently at Robyn despite their words.

She grabbed his arm and pulled him to the table where Gus, Jack, and Birdie now sat. "What do you think?" she asked him.

About everyone, including me, being unable to take our eyes off you? About how your smile warms me better than any fire? About how my heart—heck, my everything—doesn't feel right when you're not near?

"I think the Denver stage is lucky because of its name. You make everything better."

The flare of her smile held him spellbound until he glimpsed the unfamiliar flutter of her skirt as she gracefully claimed a chair at his family's table.

He crossed his arms and widened his stance, fighting the temptation to join her. "We must return to Denver. Right now."

"You're leaving?" Jack scowled at him. "After a year and a half away, why can't you stay for a day or two?"

He battled the urge to give in to his brother or admit he couldn't catch a train at this late hour or even probably find a horse to hire to ride home. He'd built too much in Denver to give it up. Even for a day, as Jack asked. "You know why. You've been in this business as long as me. There's always work to be done."

Jack's gaze dropped to his plate. Birdie's darted to her husband, and Gus' rose to study the ceiling while he tapped his chin.

Robyn stared him straight in the eye. "Tell me, what are my brothers doing in Denver?"

"They're working." Was she still concerned about them?

She didn't appear worried. Determination sharpened her steel-blue eyes. "And with them looking after your business, what's the rush to leave?"

"We're needed in Denver."

"We are and we aren't." Her bluntness made him flinch. At least she'd said *we*, not *you* or *I*.

He hadn't lost her completely. They still had a connection. One he couldn't grasp. "I don't understand."

"I know. You and my brothers don't realize that they need a change as much as anyone. They need to take the reins, to be leaders. So—" She drew in a deep breath. "I could *wish* for many things this Christmas, but this is all I will *ask* of you. If you want to give my brothers—and me—a gift, give them this time to stand on their own."

Max's shoulders hunched. He'd forgotten about Christmas gifts. "But I—" If he didn't get her out of Noelle as quickly as possible, he faced a greater chance of losing her.

"That's a mighty fine gift to ask fer 'n to give," Gus said. "Selfless on both sides."

"Agreed." Max sat defeated at the table.

Jack inhaled sharply. "You're staying?"

"Only until Christmas Day." That's when Robyn's brothers said she'd return to Denver if she hadn't made a success of her transformation. If she hadn't found the man she wanted to marry.

"That's perfect." Robyn pulled her chair closer to him.

Her proximity thrilled and then tormented his heart. How would he bear it if one day she chose to sit next to someone else?

"You won't be bored in Noelle," Jack said. "It's a bustling town now. You'll have lots to see on your holiday."

Max felt his jaw drop. "*Holiday*?" He couldn't remember the last time he or Jack had taken one. "Are you closing your office for Christmas?"

"Well..." Jack rubbed the back of his neck. "No. I have too much to do."

Max's spine stiffened. "And I don't?"

Birdie reached across the table and caught his hand. "Don't think of it as a holiday, but as a break to achieve something different." The intensity in her grip and her voice startled him. "A time to invest in what you truly need."

Right now, he needed one thing. Robyn in his life. He wanted her back in Denver with him. He'd consent to give her brothers an opportunity to change, but he couldn't give her the same chance. He also had an understanding with her brothers—do everything to stop Robyn from marrying someone who'd keep her in Noelle.

The pull of too many forces rearranging a life he'd grown comfortable with put him on edge.

"Don't glower," Robyn said. "It's only for a few days, and we can tackle Noelle together."

He latched onto the word *together*. He wasn't letting her out of his sight.

"We'll have fun," she insisted.

Not if he accomplished what he'd come to Noelle to do. His gut rolled with reprimand. One selfless act did not forgive a supremely selfish one.

Birdie squeezed his hand, dragging his focus away from his gloomy thoughts. Leaning across the table, she now grasped Robyn's hand as well as his and formed a bridge between them.

Despite their many shared conversations and smiles, he'd never had the bravery to hold Robyn's hand.

"We should go home to Peregrines' Post." Jack's gaze shot to Birdie, then Robyn.

Robyn scanned the room until she found a woman helping Nacho serve the diners. Or maybe it was the other way 'round?

"Fina looks busy. I'll talk to her tomorrow. Let me finish my taco before we go." Robyn fixed her attention on her food, and so did Birdie.

Gus grinned. "Robyn's staying in yer old room, Maximilian Boy, so you'll be bunking with me."

Max grimaced, recalling Gus' snoring. "Or I can find a room at—" He waved his hand in the air. "Does the Golden Nugget still offer room rentals?"

"Suspect they're full," Gus said. "And the new Creary Boardinghouse too."

"We won't hear of you staying with others. We'll set up a bed on our main floor." Jack gave him a clandestine wink. "Where it's quieter." He nudged his plate in front of Max. "You must be hungry. Eat this."

Jack's big brother I'll-tell-you-what's-best manner irked Max, but his belly picked that moment to rumble, so he chose to eat rather than argue.

"Yer all set 'n so am I." Gus polished off his dinner and patted his stomach happily. "I'm gonna go talk to some friends about a Christmas project."

Jack exhaled wearily before he asked much too casually, "Who are you hoping to see?"

"Ezra 'n Jasper."

The name Jasper was unfamiliar, but Ezra Thornton was not. "Is Ezra still living on the ranch with his grandson?"

"Yep. And, like me, he has a fine new granddaughter. Unfortunately, Storm's bride came with a not so fine goose." Gus shuddered.

"It's pretty late for traveling," Jack said.

"And much too dark," Max added.

Gus' expression turned puzzled, then miffed. "Who said anything about going there tonight? I'm headin' to the saloon. If I can't find Ezra or Jasper there, I can enjoy a beer or some of that whiskey Seamus 'n Norah started brewing this spring."

"Sounds like fun." Robyn set her fork on her now empty plate. "Max and I will go with you."

"We will?" He shoved his plate away from him, his appetite gone. There'd be even more men in the saloon than in the diner.

"Gus wants to talk to his friends. I want to talk to Norah.

You might find an old acquaintance you'd like to talk to as well."

He shook his head. *I only want to talk to you.*

"You'd rather go to the freight office with Jack and Birdie than to the saloon with Grandpa Gus and me?" Disappointment lowered her voice but not her gaze.

"No. I'm going with you."

Her expression brightened, but only briefly. "If you keep shaking your head like that, it might fall off."

He went completely still as he imagined her brothers doling out that advice when she was young. The thought of not having her near to challenge him made him shudder. He strove for a reply that wouldn't reveal his turmoil. "I can't figure out why the name Norah sounds familiar. I don't remember meeting her."

"She's Seamus' wife," Jack said.

The name suddenly fit. Seamus had been married before coming to Noelle. "She's the one he talked about arranging to bring to Noelle."

Robyn raised her chin. "She's *the one* who stopped waiting for him to make those arrangements. She came to Noelle on her own, and now they're a happy couple."

"You've met them?" Had she already been to the saloon? How many men had she talked to there? Had she enjoyed speaking with any of them?

"Not yet, but I want to." She fiddled with the end of her braid. "I've heard Norah has hair like mine."

"No one has hair like yours," he objected.

Robyn's eyes widened in surprise, then narrowed. "You're right. Mine's curlier than most. Redder too. Other women have better hair."

"No," he said flatly, rejecting her words.

"No?" she queried. "No, what?"

He struggled for a reply that wouldn't be boorish or bossy. Talking to her had once been so easy, but now... All he could think to say was *no*.

"You're behaving strangely. Are you feeling well?" When Robyn's gaze examined his face, her frown grew. "You look flushed. Maybe you should go to Peregrines and rest, after all."

Gus rapped the table with his knuckles. "He doesn't need sleep. He needs to *wake up* 'n say what I said earlier about not changing to please others."

When had Gus said that? Max sat taller in his chair. The 'when' didn't matter. Gus' advice was sound and reminded him of Brynmor's. *Keep insisting Rob doesn't have to change.*

"You don't need to wear a dress," he blurted.

Her frown disappeared. "You noticed my dress."

"Of course." Every man in the diner had noticed.

She smiled as she ran her hand over her skirt. "Birdie picked the fabric and the style. It's remarkable how she can take a boring bit of cloth and transform it into something... worthy of attention." She peeked at him through her lashes. "Don't you think so?"

He clenched his jaw, unable to say the truth. That the dress, like Robyn, was perfect. It fit her like a glove and was the best color to highlight her hair and freckles. He struggled to find something negative about the garment, other than the fact that it drew too many men's attention to her.

Which it continued to do as Robyn kept fidgeting with the fabric. Dealing with it appeared to take some effort.

He yanked his gaze away from her hand as she touched the curve of her waist. "Did you wear it on your ride to Noelle?"

"Yes, and that resulted in some challenges." She glared

at her skirt and shrugged. "I'm learning to work around them."

"That isn't right. You shouldn't have to work so hard."

Robyn gaped at him like he'd transformed into an unrecognizable version of himself. So, did Gus and Jack.

Only Birdie acted unfazed. "*Grand-père.*" She rose to her feet, and Jack jumped up to join her. "Remember not to stray too far from Robyn's side. She's a resourceful woman, but Noelle can bewilder..." Her gaze remained on Gus, but Max felt her words directed at him. "Recent returnees as easily as newcomers. We want to see all of you return safely to Peregrines' Post tonight."

The underlying reminder that his grandfather was prone to forgetful wandering wasn't lost on Max. Birdie had phrased her messages similarly when she'd brought Gus to Denver.

"Stay together," Jack said more bluntly. "We'll pay our bill here and expect to see you at home soon."

Gus offered his elbow to Robyn. She linked arms with him and headed for the door. Max's lips parted with wonder. He'd never seen her touch anyone so easily. Robyn disliked hugging and handshakes and... That's why he'd never been brave enough to hold out his hand to her.

He hadn't wanted to make her uncomfortable.

He scrambled to his feet and followed her—mesmerized as always by the way she moved, the straight line of her shoulders, the angle of her chin, and the sway of her hips now enhanced by the infernally perfect dress.

He didn't need it to remind him how enticing she was. She'd captivated him from the beginning.

At least her hair remained the same. It hung down her back in a long braid. If she kept changing, would he be lucky enough to see it unbound and flowing free?

His spine sagged. He couldn't hope for that. He couldn't be more selfish than he'd already committed to being. No more changes for either of them. Robyn must remain as she was—perfect in every way, even when she stayed one step ahead of him and thwarted his plans. While he must remain as he was—dog bone determined to impede and unravel her plans.

Until December 25. After that, if— No, *when* they made it back to Denver together, things could be different. They could make shared plans. He'd put aside his work to see them fulfilled.

But in Noelle, he'd have no holiday. For the next three days, he had the most important work he'd ever do.

CHAPTER 5

December 22, 1877
Three days until Christmas and the party

$\mathcal{H}$olding her lantern high, Robyn hurried down the stairs linking Peregrines' second-floor bedrooms to Jack's small carpentry shop. In the pre-dawn gloom, her light bounced off the wooden legs suspended from hooks over the workbenches. The limbs' unusual positions, in the air rather than on the ground, might have been spooky to some but not to her.

She knew what had shaped this room.

She'd pestered Max and Birdie with many questions about Noelle. Birdie had a flair for describing people in detail. Max was better at outlining buildings and the roads linking them. Most days Max had only two words for his brother. Hard-working and bossy. But he'd easily expressed a thousand words or more about this room. He made Jack's workshop as comforting as it was awe-invoking.

Jack's creations, like Birdie's dresses, were works of art crafted with care and compassion. Having lost his leg in the war, Jack knew firsthand how the right replacement gave not only the gift of mobility but a chance to regain one's confidence. People shouldn't judge other people, or even rooms, by how they looked.

They shouldn't judge themselves either.

She lengthened her stride, unwilling to examine that thought too closely.

"I only have to alter a few things," she muttered to herself, "and then I'll be happy." The naïve simplicity of her statement made her lurch to a halt.

Life was seldom simple.

The papers attached to the limbs fluttered in the wake of her sudden stop. Letters of introduction, Jack's replies requesting measurements, all the back-and-forth correspondence necessary to ensure an artificial replacement was a success.

Without the knitted liners that had previously been custom-made for each limb. Max had stopped creating them when he'd given up almost everything to pursue the dream of running his own freight office.

Pondering that loss made her spirits plummet. Had she been wrong to request that Max give her brothers the opportunity to run his business for a few days? They could be as determined as Max when they finally set their sights on something. What would they give up in order to rise to this new challenge?

She'd hoped they'd release the past and reach for the future. She didn't, however, want them to become so obsessed that they did only one thing. Like Max had done. Until he'd come back to Noelle and agreed to stay until Christmas.

Careful not to make a sound, she set her palm on the door in front of her. On the other side, Max lay on a bunk that Jack had set up for him in the freight office.

Had he slept well?

She hadn't. She'd tossed and turned with thoughts of him being so close. She'd never stayed overnight in the same building as him.

Back home, her brothers worried if she was even a minute late returning. Home currently was a one room rental over a shop where fiddles and banjos hung from the rafters.

They'd yet to see a hurdy-gurdy there. She prayed they never saw one again. While Brynmor couldn't pass the store window without looking for that instrument or for something more unobtainable—the singer who played it. They'd last seen her in Cheyenne, when Robyn's family and Lark's troupe parted ways under the order of Lark's rifle.

Proving that some musicians were as incapable of change as some freighters.

She shouldn't disturb Max if he still slept. She pressed her ear to the door and listened. All was quiet. Upstairs, Gus' infamous snoring, which Max had used many words to describe, couldn't be heard down here. The hour was too early even for early risers like Jack and Birdie.

She should go back to bed, but she was already dressed and wide awake. She'd come this far. She might as well see if Max was up. If he wasn't, she'd go upstairs and count sheep.

She turned down the wick on her lantern and eased the door open a crack.

Max's bed was empty. Her heart raced with anticipation.

She didn't have to wait. They could talk about what would happen today. She wanted him to accompany her to Cobb's Penn.

She pushed the door wide open and froze. The office was empty. Panic squeezed her chest. Had Max gone back to Denver? Had he even been in Noelle? Was last night a dream?

She shook her head at her foolishness and inhaled a fortifying breath. Max's makeshift bed was here. With his travel sack beside it.

He hadn't gone far. He'd promised to stay in Noelle until Christmas.

She'd find him in town.

She raised her chin. When she did, she'd give him something extra fine to see. Her new hair *and* her new hat. Like her brothers, she needed to let go of the past. Just a little. She'd wear Daphne's hat and keep Max's wool cap in her pocket. Same as how Brynmor kept their pa's hat in his.

Her dress had created a ripple, but she required a wave.

She strode down the meticulously straight row dividing the tidy stacks of freight. The passageway in the waist-high counter was propped open. She sailed through, set her lantern on the stovetop, and contemplated the last pieces of wood. She'd have to go outside and fetch more from the piles flanking the office. Piles stacked taller than her.

Jack had invested considerable time ensuring Birdie was well provided for.

The front door opened, and Max came in, balancing a bundle of wood in his arms. The wind had blown his blond hair into a snarl around his rugged face and neatly trimmed red beard. As always, this intoxicating combination of untamed mountain man and precise businessman drew her to him.

She rushed forward to help him.

He easily closed the door behind him with his heel. He, of course, didn't need her for something as simple as that.

He was a capable man used to living on his own. But she couldn't stop wanting to be part of his life, and he spent most of his time working.

"Let me take some of that wood," she said.

A frown pinched his brow. "Better not. Wouldn't want to get your dress dirty." He steered a wide path around her and unloaded his wood by the stove. Dropping to one knee, he began arranging the pile in a neat stack.

She planted her hands on her hips. "Women who wear dresses can still make fires, you know."

"I've no doubt of that." His frown deepened when he stopped to stare at her dress.

She felt her cheeks grow hot. His face appeared rosier as well. That was probably from his recent trip outside in the invigorating air. Without even a shred of a smile, hoping he was finally looking at her in a new way was foolish.

"But when I worked in this office," he said in a gruffer than usual voice as he went back to his stacking, "my first task was starting the fire while Jack started the coffee." He glanced at the pot sitting on the stovetop, and his tone lightened. "It's a sad fact, but no amount of practice will make anything I brew as good as his." He flashed her a smile that melted the stiffness from her body. "Or yours."

"You're such a tease. You and my brothers." She stomped her foot, but couldn't help grinning. She'd missed their banter. "You just want me to cook for you."

He chuckled. "Yes and no. I'm hoping you'll make us some coffee. That's all. Your brothers are angling for you to cook more of the meals."

"They've been doing that for a long time. But they're better cooks than me. At least Bryn is."

"That's the older sibling's cross to bear," Gus grumbled.

Robyn whipped around to find Max's grandfather

watching them from a perch on a stool behind the post office end of the counter.

"Yer brothers are worried the wheels on the wagon will stop rollin' if they ain't on top of it. So, they do the stuff *others* don't want to do 'n not always what *they* want to do. Which ain't right." He thrust his finger in the air. "Seize the day 'n do what you want, I say!"

The return of Max's frown made her hesitant to discuss her plans. So, like a coward, she asked, "What's on your list for today, *Bon-papa?*"

Gus crossed his arms. "Can't tell you. It's a secret."

Max's cough drew her attention.

He held her gaze as he tapped his chest and tilted his head back toward Gus. The tips of several knitting needles protruded from under Gus' tweed vest.

"Late to bed and early to rise," Max whispered to her.

"The traits of a man on a mission," Robyn replied in the same tone.

Gus winked at them. "That's me."

"*That*," Max said with a sigh, "is what worries me."

She shared his concerns plus one of her own. She hoped Max's arrival in Noelle had ended Gus' urge to introduce her to every bachelor in Noelle.

Last night, Gus had found Jasper but not Ezra in the Golden Nugget Saloon. The two old-timers had claimed a corner table where they conversed covertly. Max and Robyn sat at the bar and chatted with Norah and Seamus—whenever the couple weren't pulled away to tend customers.

The saloon had been as full as the diner. She hoped today wasn't as busy. She wanted to get to know all of the Noelle women better.

Norah, similar to Fina, had been a whirlwind at work. She'd also been willing to put aside her labors this morning and ask Cara to do the same. They'd meet her at Avis' store to discuss hats and hair.

The closer that event came, the more nervous she became.

"Time to seize the day," she mumbled as she reached for the pot on the stove. "I'll get the coffee brewing."

"I'll add more wood to the fire." Max worked beside her in silence, but when they all had steaming mugs in their hands, he spoke instead of drinking. "What time are you expected at Cobb's Penn?"

His surprisingly direct question made her choke on her coffee. She sputtered her reply. "As—soon as—it—opens."

Norah was eager to, as she'd said in her delightfully lilting Irish accent, compare hair horror stories with her and Cara.

"That's perfect."

"It is?" His certainty puzzled her.

"Yes. Jack and Birdie will be down soon. There'll be time to discuss Noelle's shipping before you head out. You were always interested in every end of the business. Maybe you aren't now."

Her confusion deepened. "Of course, I am. Why wouldn't I be?"

"Last night you spoke of other things." He pinched the bridge of his nose. "Mostly shopping and socializing."

He made her sound frivolous. He made her feel guilty. Her shoulders slumped. Max's expression turned as glum as her mood.

She enjoyed talking to people, but the shopping was only a means to an end. Hauling freight had made her happy until she wanted more. With Max. "Jack said you could take a holiday." *Why won't you take that holiday? With me?*

"And Birdie said..." Gus tapped the counter impatiently. "Something similar. Something 'bout investin' time in what you truly need."

His words raised her spirits. She was relieved to have him as her ally again. "You're right, *Bon-papa*, that's exactly what Birdie said."

Max stared at his cup. He hadn't taken a drink, which was odd. In Denver, he'd always enjoyed her coffee. In Noelle, things were different. And not the different she'd hope for.

He adjusted his hold on his cup. "Jack also said he had too much work to take a holiday. I'm only suggesting we spend a few minutes listening to his plans for the day before we go about ours."

Gus huffed. "Talkin' about work usually leads to gettin' involved in work."

Max nodded, but when he caught her watching him, he went unusually still.

"Well, I got my own project to attend to." Gus downed a large swig of coffee and smacked his lips in appreciation. "Can't dillydally. Not even over this good a treat. I'm off to Ezra's as soon as my cup is empty."

Max's spine stiffened as his gaze pinned his grandfather. "You're not planning to go to Ezra's ranch on your own."

"Of course, I am. Why shouldn't I?" Gus held up his hand. "Don't answer that. I've heard it all from yer brother. *What happens if you wander off the road? Or you fall down the mountain?* Even Birdie knows better than to do that now. This ain't like last winter when she—"

"*Bon-papa*, we invited Jasper to join us here for breakfast."

Gus slurped another mouthful of coffee. "When'd you do that?"

"Last night. It wasn't only me, it was—"

"That was mighty nice of you." Gus raised his cup to his lips again.

"Max suggested it first, but *we all* agreed."

"Oh." Gus lowered his hand. "It's coming back to me now. Jasper 'n me are gonna talk to Ezra together."

"That's the plan." Max finally drank from his cup. "And everything will be fine if we follow the plan."

Robyn frowned. Plans were only the first step. She'd made a lot of them and they'd yet to yield even a glimmer of her desired outcome. If Max accompanied her to Cobb's Penn and witnessed her next transformation, but then continued to treat her as oddly as he had since seeing her in a dress... Well, then everything was definitely not fine. It meant her worst fears might be happening.

She'd changed not only herself but Max. In all the wrong ways. She was losing her best friend.

CHAPTER 6

*R*obyn stole another glance out Cobb's Penn's window, hoping to see Max striding down Noelle's main street toward the general store—and her.

When Jasper had not appeared for breakfast, their plans had careened off the rails. Gus had been determined to find his missing friend. No one could fault him for that. She'd offered to delay her arrival at Cobb's Penn and join his search. Gus had refused her help, saying Max's assistance would be sufficient.

The two men had departed Peregrines' Post, each carrying a burlap sack of wool—but only after Max clandestinely transferred half of Gus' load to his and vowed he'd join her at Cobb's Penn as soon as he could.

That'd been a while ago. Max should be here by now. Unless they hadn't found Jasper. Then they did need her help. Choosing to pursue her own goals rather than assisting the people who mattered most in her life made her stomach churn with self-reprimand.

"Are you all right?" Avis inquired.

She gave up trying to appear sophisticated and nonchalant in front of the shop owner as well as Norah and Cara. "I'm worried about Gus' friend. Jasper was supposed to join us for breakfast." She moved as close as she could to the window without disturbing the many items on display and scanned the street. "Max and Gus are searching for him. I should've gone with them."

"Ease your mind," Norah said. "Jasper's fine. I saw him looking after one of the orphans who arrived earlier this month." Norah laughed. "In a corner of our saloon, no less. His complete devotion to the challenge sprung upon him so unexpectedly was adorable."

"This town needs a nursery." Avis' tone turned disgruntled. "Tending a baby can wear down even the stoutest of hearts and bodies."

Cara gave her a reassuring look. "Jasper can handle more than most."

Robyn heaved a sigh of relief, then acceptance. Jasper wasn't lost. He'd merely been too distracted to join them for breakfast. That also meant Jasper couldn't accompany Gus to Ezra's home. Max would've taken up the task. He couldn't join her until he'd traveled to the Thornton ranch and back.

"You're right, Cara," Norah said with a wry chuckle. "Leave it to an old-timer to show us some Christmas spirit. The entire town could learn a lot from his generosity."

Avis huffed. "We all need to help each other more."

Robyn turned away from the window to face her trio of helpers. "Thank you for agreeing to help me."

"It's our pleasure," Cara said.

"And it'll be fun," Norah assured her.

"Shall we style your hair before we choose your hat?" Avis asked.

When she nodded, Avis pulled a chair into the center of the room and gestured for her to sit.

After she did, the three women formed a semi-circle in front of her.

Norah rubbed her palms together. "Let's have a look." She gestured for Robyn to remove her wool cap.

Robyn did so slowly and held it in her lap.

Cara gave her a curious look. "Can't blame you for being reluctant to take off your hat. It's lovely."

She played the fabric through her fingers. "Max knitted it for me."

"Oh." Cara drew out the word, slowly and knowingly. "I see."

"Yes," Norah said. "I saw a lot last night too."

Robyn glanced up to find the two redheads grinning at her. Her shoulders slumped. "Am I being that obvious?"

"You're being you, and we"—Avis gave Cara and Norah a chastising look—"having each longed for someone we thought we couldn't have, shouldn't tease you."

"Quite right." Norah sighed. "Last night after you left the Nugget, Seamus mentioned that Max had a talent many in Noelle teased him about."

Robyn frowned. The Max she knew didn't seem particularly disturbed by any kind of teasing. He appeared too confident to care what others said. The last time she'd seen him really perturbed was when her brothers first called him Dog Bone.

"Would Max knit more caps?" Avis asked. "We could sell them at Cobb's Penn."

Cara laughed. "You're always looking for new stock."

"Having people make things in town makes it easier to keep our shelves full." Avis' gaze cut to Robyn. "Don't get me wrong. The Peregrines always do their best transporting our goods. And now that the railroad's reached town, shipments from Denver are even faster. But imagine having everything made in town."

"Or even a few more things. We're lucky to have Birdie's dresses, Daphne's hats, Jolie and Hank's gift cards, Victoria's baking and Alejandro's sweets, and"—Cara winked at Norah —"your and Seamus' whiskey."

The same question that she'd asked the Peregrines last night rose in her mind. "Do you think anyone else would wear my cap?"

Cara started undoing Robyn's braid. "There's something for everyone. Look at the wooden legs Jack creates. Luckily, most people don't need them, but those who do are very lucky to receive them."

"But would any *woman* wear my cap?"

Avis brought out a hairbrush. "Of course, you're wearing it."

"I meant, would *other* women?"

Cara tilted her head as she considered the question. "Anything made of wool would be handy for our cold weather."

Avis examined Robyn's face. "Your skin could use some help in that area." She handed the brush to Norah. "Get to work while I check my inventory."

"Can you remove my freckles?" Robyn asked.

Norah huffed as she commenced briskly brushing Robyn's hair. "Avis won't stock those kinds of products."

"Because they do more harm than good." Avis shook her finger at them as she strode to a shelf of neatly arranged jars. "All freckles are beautiful. Robyn's skin only requires soothing from the frost and wind." She selected a jar and handed it to Cara. "Apply this while I gather my hairpins and ribbons."

"You'll soon have skin as soft as..." Norah laughed. "Your cap."

"Wool usually makes me itchy." Cara touched Robyn's cap before she began applying the lotion to Robyn's skin, which, as promised, brought instant relief. "Why is your cap different?"

"It starts with the sheep," she replied. "A family from Spain are raising a special breed near Denver."

"Denver, Denver, Denver," Avis muttered as she laid a dazzling rainbow of hair ribbons on the nearest counter. "Why can't someone start a similar farm closer to Noelle?"

Norah's brushing stopped. "Maybe Max could."

The mention of his name sent Robyn's gaze skittering to the window, where she still saw no sign of him joining her.

"Yes, he's a knitter," Avis said. "So, he knows about wool, but it sounds like you do as well, Robyn."

Cara grabbed her hand. "You and Max could stay in Noelle and raise sheep and sell knitted items and—" Cara released her. "Why are you shaking your head so vehemently?"

"We enjoy freighting too much to give it up. It's what brought us together." It was what kept them together until she'd left Denver and disrupted their connection.

Norah resumed her brushing. "Working with a partner can be rewarding. You mentioned your brothers were also involved in freighting."

"Would one of them be interested in something new?" Cara asked.

The steady stroke of Norah's brush raised a memory. Bryn had done this when she was little. His big hands hadn't been so agile. He'd fumbled a lot and muttered many curses, but he'd taken up the brush every night until she claimed the task as her own. Her memories were full of many similar events. Her big brothers bending their backs and their lives to help not only her but others.

If a task needed doing, they did it. But what did they *really* enjoy doing?

She tried to imagine them herding sheep. Heddwyn's craving for speed and Griffin's need to be in the middle of things didn't fit a farm's slower pace and isolation. That left Brynmor. "My oldest brother might." But Bryn would never let anyone split up their family.

"Will he be joining you in Noelle? Does he need a bride?" Cara grinned. "Noelle's matchmakers will be keen to meet him."

She doubted their interest would last long. Bryn's size intimidated most people. His clouded eye had become the real conversation killer. Or worse. Heaven help anyone who asked how it had happened. "Brynmor's...extra busy in Denver while Max and I are away. All of my brothers are."

Cara closed her jar of lotion. "They must miss you, and you them."

"But..." She strove to find a bright side for her brothers as well. "I believe we all needed a change."

Norah circled her, touching her hair lightly as she did. "Don't change too much."

"Why not?"

Avis took the jar and brush from Cara and Norah and set them on the counter beside the hair ribbons and pins. "Because then you won't be you."

"And we like you," Cara folded her arms decisively.

Norah and Avis mimicked her stance. The three women stood in a row. Facing Robyn. United. Her brothers did the same when they were worried or being protective.

The women in Denver had done the opposite. They shied away from her. Peered over their shoulders at her. They never acted like friends.

A lump rose in her throat. Would she be lucky enough to see these women after she left Noelle? Or even after she left this shop?

Some friendships were doomed from the start. Lark and her songbird sisters had shown Robyn that. But even if friendships couldn't last, they could still be enjoyed—in the moment.

Happiness was a gift, one that could be received or given...or even better, shared.

She squared her shoulders. "Styling my hair can easily be undone, right?"

When they shrugged noncommittally, she flashed the grin she'd used to sway her brothers and Gus. "And trying on hats... That's something we could do together, right?"

"Oh!" Cara clapped her hands. "You are *so* right."

"We can select hats for each other as well as for ourselves." Norah waved for them to follow her.

Robyn left her chair and joined them by Daphne's hat display.

Avis passed out hand mirrors. "I hope we have time to try on all of the hats."

They all nodded. *Time.* That was another gift.

While her new friends hovered around her, chatting happily and placing hats on each other's heads, including hers—she stole one last peek out the window.

Max still hadn't appeared. He'd taken the time to join her in Noelle, but how much happiness could they share if they spent less and less time together? And how much time would anyone want to spend with her if she weren't happy?

No one enjoyed being near miserable people. But even the smallest of smiles could lead to laughter.

She put her wool cap in her skirt pocket and tried to be happy without Max. Maybe then they'd have a better chance of being happy together when they next met.

CHAPTER 7

$\mathcal{M}$ax scowled at the horses' backs, the buckboard beneath his feet, his hands holding the lines. He flicked them again, encouraging the pair of grays to increase their pace. After more than a year away, he was back doing what he'd done every day in Noelle. Putting out fires for his brother's business.

Jack's mantra rang in his head. *Peregrines is a family business.* His big brother could be exceptionally pedantic about reminding everyone about the family involvement while in the same sentence needling Max about his obligation.

Not that Jack meant to rile him. But his words often did. And his actions, too.

Despite preaching total partnership, Jack held back information. He couldn't stop being the leader who tried to shelter his family and ended up shepherding them as well. In Denver, Max enjoyed knowing every detail. Robyn and her brothers' fondness for talk had a lot to do with that, but there was more. He was in the middle of their work. He was in charge of his destiny.

Lord knew what would happen today in Noelle. That was the Noelle way. Out of his control.

As usual, his family and everyone here had a knack for blasting all of his plans to smithereens. His campaign to find a minder for Gus, so he could stay close to Robyn, had developed more snags than a river full of fallen trees. His grandfather had become exceptionally wily in his quest to pursue his independence and his latest project.

Knitting. He snorted. He knew from experience that no one here valued it. At least it was now keeping Gus occupied with Ezra.

Another crafty old-timer. He snorted again. He hadn't been able to refuse Ezra's request that he drive this load of hay bales from the Thornton ranch to the train depot. A farm down the line needed the feed, and the Thorntons had a surplus, *and* Ezra's grandson was busy. Doing heaven knew what. He hadn't seen Storm at the ranch.

He'd seen a goose who behaved like a watchdog, however. He rubbed the sore spot on his leg where the beast had pecked him. He would've gladly taken the bird to market as well, but apparently it was a pet.

Yep, no doubt about it. Noelle was out of control.

He exhaled a relieved breath when he finally reached the familiar curve in the road—with its unfamiliar book-store and bakery on his left. He executed the turn onto the main street, threading his way through riders and walkers—without a break in his horses' strides.

Ha! He snapped the lines, and the team accelerated. Satisfaction surged through his veins. Sitting in an office pushing paper had not dulled his driving skills, as Robyn's brothers often teased.

Cobb's Penn's storefront came up fast. Faster than a new plan could form in his brain. How would he convince Robyn to abandon her transformation inside and spend her time with him outside?

She could help him with his cargo. Wearing a dress? Why not? The Robyn he knew could do anything.

He halted the team, yanked the wagon's handbrake, tied the horses to the hitching rail, and bounded onto the boardwalk. He slowed only to peer through the window. A cluster of people stood inside. Their proximity to one another and his pace made individual identification impossible. A flash of red made his spirit rejoice, then rebel.

Neither the length nor the shade was right. Had they changed Robyn's hair so much he wouldn't recognize her?

He yanked open the door. It hit the wall with a bang.

Three dark-haired women turned to face him, revealing all of the person—and not only the top of their head—who previously stood behind the group. Liam Fulton. The red-haired man who owned the shop.

Robyn wasn't here.

"Sorry for the disturbance." He spun on his heel to make his exit.

"Hold up, Max!" Liam strode toward him, grabbed his hand, and shook it enthusiastically. "It's good to see you back in Noelle. My wife, Avis"—he gestured to the woman who'd left the others and walked toward him as well—"was just telling me about your knitting."

"My..." He trailed off in confusion. He must not have heard correctly. "There's been a mistake." *I don't do that anymore.* "I only run freight."

Liam's wife closed the door and stood in front of it, blocking his departure. "I saw the cap you made for Robyn."

"She was here." Max scanned the shop again, feeling idiotic because obviously she had been and had now gone elsewhere. "Did she return to Peregrines?"

"Went across the street to Nacho's." Liam looped his arm around his wife and gazed down at her affectionately. "I think my arrival disrupted your party. But at least your new friend left with ribbons in her hair and a fine hat on her head."

Avis' dark eyes studied Max closely. "She left happy."

He flinched. "She was...smiling?"

"A lot," Avis replied without hesitation. "She also talked a lot about dance lessons."

And Robyn was now inside the diner, the dancing lady's domain. His spine sagged. "I'm too late."

"I'd say you're right on time." Liam slapped him on the shoulder. "Avis was wondering if you could make more of your caps? With some sort of special wool? We'd like to try selling them here."

"I can't. Gus has—" He buttoned his lip.

Gus had taken the knitting needles Max had left at Peregrines, and he could keep them. He also deserved to keep his activities secret until he, and only he, wished to reveal them.

Alarm widened Avis' eyes, and Liam's too as he asked, "Is your grandfather missing again? Do you need our help finding him?"

Their concern for his grandfather startled, then comforted him. There were good people in Noelle, but that didn't mean it was a good place for him to stay.

"Gus is fine. He's working. I need to return to my work as well." He pointed to the door behind Avis and Liam. "I've a delivery waiting outside."

Liam opened the door. "Come see us when you're done."

"And we'll talk about your knitting more." Avis stepped aside, and his path was finally clear.

"Can't," he muttered as he strode out and reclaimed his seat on the wagon. "I'm too busy."

"Hope you're not too busy to attend Noelle's Christmas Party." Avis' words followed him down the street as he set the wagon rolling, at a much slower pace than before.

The diner and Robyn were behind him now. He was too late to stop her dancing lessons. He turned the next corner and headed for the bridge in a stupor. He didn't want to go forward. He wanted to go back.

All the way back to his days working with Robyn in Denver and his nights...dreaming about holding her in his arms. A jolt of excitement made him sit up straight. The team, sensing the change in him, sped up.

Today he had a chance to hold Robyn for real. As soon as he unloaded this wagon, raced back to the diner, and cut in on the dance partner currently holding her. Jealously made him pull back on the lines.

The team snorted and tossed their heads, confused by his mixed signals.

He locked his gaze on the train depot ahead and mapped the shortest path to the best location to unload his cargo as fast as possible. A partially loaded wagon rested next to an open railcar. He parked beside it and started heaving bales into the empty side of the car.

"No time even for a hello, I see," drawled a familiar voice.

He glanced over to see his brother setting a crate on the wagon bed opposite him. He scanned Jack's wagon, but the only other familiar sight was the Peregrines' team of mules.

"Where's Woody?" he asked, eager for their friend's help.

"Busy with his menagerie of animals, I imagine." Jack stepped back inside the railcar.

And Max went back to throwing bales onto the side his brother had conveniently emptied for him to fill.

Jack came out carrying another crate. "No need to rush. This train doesn't leave for a few minutes. And I'll help you unload your wagon soon as I'm done loading mine."

Not if I get done first. Then I'll be helping you. He tossed the bales faster. He paused only to jump aboard the railcar and stack the hay along the wall to make room for more. Then he was back on his wagon and repeating the routine.

It allowed him to enter another routine. Talking to his brother in stops and starts as they worked.

"I heard Woody got married."

Jack disappeared inside the railcar and only answered when he came out with his next crate. "He did."

"Happily so?" Max asked as he prepared to leap into the car. "Very."

Jealousy upset his balance. He fell on the bales and scrambled upright, hoping Jack hadn't seen.

"You all right?" Jack called from outside.

"I'm fine." He should have been more than fine. Woody was a good man. So were Nacho, Seamus, Storm, and Liam. And his brother, too. He should've been happy to hear and see them settled.

"Woody drives the stagecoach sometimes." Jack's words distracted him from his moody thoughts.

"But he no longer drives your freight wagons?"

"He's too busy." Jack winced as his own stride finally faltered. He paused long enough to rub his thigh above his wooden leg before going back to work.

"And you aren't?" And if Woody wasn't helping Jack, who was?

"The work here is my responsibility. And I don't mind

being with the mules now. I even like that one." Jack gestured to the mule on the right.

Which looked identical to the mule on the left, but Max knew the difference. The mule Jack *liked* had helped him save Birdie from falling off the side of the mountain to her death.

"Gus is with Ezra now?" Jack asked, ever the worrier.

"Yep. And he said he'd be busy there the whole day. Didn't want to be disturbed until supper time—when he'd make his own way home."

"I'm good with the first part of that scenario. Not the last."

"Same here."

They worked in silence for a full minute as Max mulled over another topic. Noelle's matchmakers and their successes.

"So...Storm is happily married as well?"

"He is. You didn't see him and Molly at their ranch?"

"I was in a hurry to get back to town." He scowled. "I saw her goose, however."

Jack laughed. "The gander's name is Daniel."

Max laughed with him. And his mood lightened. When had he last laughed with his brother? "Noelle is a crazy place."

"But a good place, too. Or it's trying to be." His brother paused briefly again to rub his thigh. "We had a lot of strife that came with the railroad construction."

"Ezra told me the best spot to put down roots is near a town, but not in it." But when Max had last lived in Noelle, he remembered Ezra worrying that the Thorntons' ranch might not be a good fit for him and his grandson. Their house was too big for just the two of them.

As if reading his mind, Jack said, "Ezra also says the best only came after Molly moved into their house."

"Why haven't you built—?" He bit back the words *a house for you and Birdie*.

Not enough time would be the answer. Time was the eternal problem.

"Do you have plans after supper?" Jack's smile remained firmly in place.

Max's good humor vanished. "I hoped to spend my evening with Robyn." But if he didn't make it to Nacho's and make a good impression there, she might not want to speak to him later.

A frown shrouded Jack's happiness. "You should be with her right now. I should've taken Gus to Ezra's and been the one to haul those hay bales. Let me finish unloading them while you go find Robyn."

Relief flooded Max. He jumped down from his wagon and turned toward town—where he saw Culver Daniels running toward them. For a big man, the blacksmith moved remarkably fast. He reminded Max of the Llewellyn brothers. Except he wasn't a redhead or Welsh or a man prone to teasing others.

Culver grabbed his hand and shook it as heartily as Liam had. "Good to see you two working together again. Makes it easier to ask for your help. I know you're busy. You're always busy, but I have a pair of sculptures I need to get on this train."

Max stifled his groan. "That's a two-man job."

"Even faster done by three," Culver said. "It'll be like old times. The Peregrine family saving the day."

Maybe in Noelle, but not in the war, where they'd first met Culver. They'd known him longer than anyone in

Noelle. Max couldn't refuse him. "We'll need to finish here first."

Culver leapt inside the railcar. "I can assist with that." He planted his hands on his hips as he glanced between Max and Jack. And gave them the biggest grin Max had ever seen on the man's face. "*Who* needs the most help finishing?"

Surprise dropped Max's jaw. He was wrong. The smithy was a teaser as well. He'd heard Culver had also married last Christmas. Had his wife improved his humor? The man radiated joy.

Max huffed, but couldn't help joining in the torment. "Jack needs the most help. As usual, he's slower than me."

Jack let out a sigh, and the familiar worry lines returned to his brow. "You don't have to stay," he whispered between receiving crates from Culver so their conversation remained private. "You could've said no. You still can."

"Have I ever said no to work?"

"You probably should now. Robyn's—"

"Happy doing what she needs to do." Avis had said she'd been smiling a lot. "And besides helping Culver, you still need to deliver your incoming shipment to the town. And I need to return this wagon to the Thorntons."

"You'll have time to see Robyn tonight," Jack said.

"Yes, I will." And as soon as they were alone and no one could interfere, he'd ask her point blank to help with Peregrine work.

"This is the last one," Culver said as he handed a crate to Jack and turned to Max. "Now for the bales."

Max dredged up a smile. "Thanks for helping us."

"It's the least I could do, and I'll do more."

"You don't have to," Max replied. "Hauling freight is our job."

"And," Jack added, "it's our pleasure to help a friend."

"My thoughts exactly," Culver said. "I look forward to returning the favor."

Ezra had said similar. Max shrugged and tossed bales to Culver, hoping to turn the conversation to a simpler topic. Ezra and Culver's favors wouldn't help him convince Robyn to return to Denver with him.

Her brothers would be mighty disgusted if they learned of his failures today. He was disgusted with himself.

As they'd suggested, distracting Robyn with the enticement of helping with Jack's work was his best plan. And judging by how her eyes had lit up this morning when she'd peppered Jack with questions about his deliveries for the day, it should have been an easy plan to accomplish. If he cut out all the unreliable parts, like depending on Jasper to show up for breakfast, the plan could still work. He still had a chance of getting Robyn to come home to Denver with him.

Unless she had changed so much in one day that she'd lost interest in what had previously made her happy and didn't want to spend time with him anymore.

CHAPTER 8

*R*obyn set five dinner plates on the office counter and sighed. Not only in appreciation of the beautiful counter Jack built, but in commiseration for the Peregrine family not having enough room for a dining table, and in disappointment that she hadn't seen Max since breakfast.

She tentatively touched her hair arranged atop her head, the soft ribbons and hard pins holding it up. Her fingers skimmed the back of her neck, which made her shiver. Without the warm weight of her braid, she felt...exposed. She tried to distract herself by keeping her hands busy. She arranged the cutlery by the plates and placed the high stools in front of the settings.

It astounded her that Jack had built a chair just for her. That he hadn't been content merely to lend her Max's seat in the belief his brother wouldn't be here for Christmas. She sighed again. This time happily.

Jack and Birdie and Gus had made her feel like a desired part of their family.

"It's really lovely," Birdie said.

"I'm honored that Jack made a seat for me, especially since I'll only be here a few days."

"*Oui*, Jack's gifts are also *très beaux*, but I was speaking of your hair," Birdie said from her seat by the stove.

A spot Robyn had suggested because Birdie had sounded out of breath. Not that she'd told Birdie that. Instead, she'd admitted to being a terrible cook, and that Birdie had better sit and tend to the stew, or they'd be eating burnt food.

She'd come to realize that Birdie was as stubborn as Gus and as hardworking as Jack. Birdie had spent all day sewing. And in Gus' absence, she'd also run the postal counter. While Robyn gallivanted around town, changing and not changing.

Her time at Cobb's Penn had, except for Max not being there, gone according to plan. Her time with Fina afterward had not, but she'd still managed to be helpful. Now guilt pricked her conscience.

She should've helped Birdie first.

"What did the folks at Nacho's say when they saw your new hair and hat?"

"There was little time for talk." Which wasn't completely true. The diner had once again been too busy for Fina to give Robyn dance lessons. She'd stayed to help serve the customers and, as before, struggled to converse with them. "But I met Jane Creary there. She taught me how to handle the food orders."

"Thank goodness she and her family chose to stay and run their boardinghouse. After so many treated them so terribly, I wouldn't have blamed them if they'd left. The Crearys are the best of neighbors. Hardworking. Kind. Always eager to help.

"When Jane saw me struggling, she tried to help, but..."

Robyn straightened her backbone. It'd take a lot more time to teach her the art of conversing with strangers, but she must invest the time. The gift of that gab would come in handy at the Christmas party—where she still hoped to dazzle Max. "Jane said she'd ask her sister, Rosalind, for advice about talking in groups."

"There are many things to learn, but while you are learning them, know this." Birdie's spoon circled the pot at a determined pace. "You are already perfect as you are. And I'll say it again and again until you believe it. Your hair, whether in a braid or as it is now, is *très beau*. You are beautiful no matter what you wear."

Robyn appreciated Birdie's conviction, but she wasn't so certain. After returning to the office and not finding Max here, she'd stowed her new hat under her bed upstairs. It could stay there until the Christmas party. She'd felt odd wearing it at the diner and on the street. It seemed too flamboyant to wear...anywhere.

Not like her cap, which she'd been comfortable wearing everywhere. She couldn't, however, don it tonight if she wanted Max to see her newly transformed hair.

Where are you? She stared at the door, willing it to open and for Max to walk in, for all three of the Peregrine men to appear.

Only the daft, the desperate, or the devil traveled the wilderness after dusk.

In a big city with many streets, she'd never failed to find one that led home. While here in Noelle, surrounded by so much snow...

Her shivers returned. "It's getting late."

"Maybe they're across the street again?" Birdie had informed her that she'd last seen Max and Jack helping their friend Culver, the blacksmith who'd married the gypsy widow, load several hefty items onto the train.

She must know the depot's schedule well to have chanced seeing them. Or had she just looked outside a lot?

Robyn's gaze followed Birdie's to the ladder by the window.

"Keep your eyes on the stew. I'll take a look."

Birdie laughed. "Oh, the things you'll do to get out of cooking. I envy your height."

Robyn snorted because she knew Birdie was more than content with what she had, including the office's unusually high windows that made the use of a ladder necessary for Birdie to see outside. Birdie loved every inch of Peregrines' Post and Freight. She would never ask for more. But she and Jack needed more.

They needed a home away from their work and their worries. Unfortunately, Jack had been so busy doing jobs for others that he hadn't had time to build his own house.

As she approached the window, a firm knock rapped on the door and halted her in her tracks.

A stranger must be outside. Someone who, like Birdie when she'd first arrived in Noelle last year, hadn't known to open the door and let herself in. Peregrines was a business open more hours than not.

Or maybe Max waited outside carrying so much wood that this time he couldn't open the door. He needed her help.

She yanked open the door.

Revealing her brother, Heddwyn, standing on the doorstep. He'd never been to Noelle, but he'd heard the stories about Peregrines. He knew he could open the door, but he hadn't. Why?

A series of expressions crossed his face as he stared at her. Shock. Awe. Uncertainty. Terror.

Her heart seized with dread. She grabbed his arm and shook it hard. "Why are you here and not in Denver? What's wrong?"

"Thank the blessed stars, you're still you." He enveloped her in a tight hug.

She gasped for air. Why was he behaving so oddly? She could count the times on one hand that he'd hugged her. Her panic grew. She tried to wriggle free. When he wouldn't let go, she jabbed him in the ribs with her knuckles.

"Ouch!" He stepped back, rubbing his side and looking more offended than injured.

She knew this expression well, but the familiarity didn't comfort her. "Has something happened to Bryn or Griff?" she demanded.

His brows shot up, and so did his palms. "Now calm down, Little Red Robyn. Nothing's happened to anyone."

Her entire body sagged with relief. "Then why are you here?"

"Because..." He shrugged sheepishly. "Nothing happened. To anyone. In Denver."

She narrowed her gaze on him. "You came here because you were *bored*?"

"And now I'm not. The train ride was fascinating, and Noelle is mesmerizing. So tiny and strange. But the most astounding thing is this!" He waved to her hair and her dress. "You've done it. Have you received his proposal of—?"

"Not yet." Her inability to say otherwise made her scowl. "And this—" She waved at him standing in Peregrines' doorway. "Was not part of our agreement."

Hedd's lower lip protruded in a fake pout. "Could you *agree* to let your poor ol' brother inside?"

"You really should," Birdie said. "It's cold outside."

Robyn flinched. She'd forgotten about Birdie. "Get inside, Hedd. You're letting in the cold air." She yanked him in and slammed the door against the draft, concerned not for her brother's well-being but for Birdie's.

But Birdie was now smiling brightly.

Heddwyn doffed his wool cap and returned her smile. "Greetings, *Hen who Rules the Roost.* Thank you for your clucking voice of reason."

Birdie laughed. "Of all of the Llewellyn brothers, you are the most terrible of the teasers."

Robyn grasped his arm again. "Do Bryn and Griff know you're here?"

Hedd looked everywhere but at her. "Look at those dresses." He released a low whistle as he inspected Birdie's inventory hanging on several lines. "They're spectacular."

"A teaser and a flatterer." Birdie shook her head. "Heaven help the ladies of Noelle. Especially the single ones."

"No time for them. I want to see everything that you told me about this office. Like Jack's counter." He ran his hand along the length of it. "And Gus' leather tooling rack and—" He paused only to sniff the air. "Is that stew I smell? I'm famished."

Robyn folded her arms. "You're not getting any food until you answer my question."

"Bryn and Griff will hardly notice I'm gone." Hedd circled the room, examining Pearl's drawings on the walls and the white and royal blue panels that hung beneath the high windows.

Birdie had found the bird-patterned fabric, an almost identical print to the ones she sold last year, on one of her summer trips to Denver.

"There's so much to see and touch and taste." He moved to the stove. "I'm tired of my own cooking."

Birdie's gaze met hers. "It's too late for him to catch a train home."

"That's right." Hedd edged closer to the stew. "But I promise I'll board one tomorrow if you feed me tonight."

"Fine. But you'll have to wait until the Peregrine men get home."

A blush rose on Birdie's cheeks. "We don't have enough plates, or seats, for six people. I'm—" Birdie's spoon halted. "I'm sorry that I'm not a better hostess."

True guilt etched Hedd's face as stared at the counter with its limited space. Before either of them could reassure Birdie that she was a wonderful hostess, the door opened and in strode Jack.

Without Max or Gus.

Jack blinked in surprise as his gaze locked on Hedd. Then he smiled and offered his hand to shake. "You must be Heddwyn."

It was Hedd's turn to look confused. "How does he know...?" He trailed off as he glanced at Robyn and Birdie, who was grinning at her husband.

"Of course. You described me to your husband. The same way you described him to me." He grabbed Jack's hand and pumped it vigorously. "Hello, *wild-haired man who never stops working*. No, that's too long a name. You're..." He contemplated the ceiling as if deep in thought before proclaiming with a devilish smile, "Busy Bee. On account of you being so short and yellow-haired."

Jack cocked a brow as he studied her brother's height with the eye of a carpenter used to measuring everything. Hedd wasn't more than a hand's width taller than Jack and Max.

A smile twitched Jack's lips. He didn't need her to explain her brother's tomfoolery. When he winked at Birdie, Robyn knew she'd told her husband about the tomfoolery as well. "Or you could just call me Jack?"

Hedd huffed with indignation, but his eyes shone with amusement. "Where's the fun in that? You're an awful lot like your brother, you know."

"Where is he?" Robyn struggled not to let her anxiety creep into her voice. "And Gus too?"

"Max took a wagon to fetch Gus from Ezra's ranch."

"He's been out there the entire day?" Birdie's tone turned relieved. "That's good to hear. I wasn't certain where he was."

Jack frowned as he went to his wife, bent down on one knee, and gently cupped her cheek. He didn't comment on her needing to rest or not worry so much. He probably sensed he'd pestered her enough yesterday. "I'm sorry I didn't tell you sooner."

Birdie laid her hand over his and leaned into his touch. "An apology is unnecessary. There is no need to molly-coddle me, but in *Grand-père's* case... Perhaps delivering him to Ezra's ranch where he'll be content to sit and knit every day is a wise idea. At least until their project is finished."

Jack placed a kiss on Birdie's forehead, a slow one that expressed so much love it made Robyn's heart ache. Max had yet to even hold her hand.

"Could you rustle up a seat for our newest arrival?" Birdie whispered.

Jack rose to his feet. "Begin dinner without me. I'll be back in a flash." He scowled at the counter as he lifted the passageway that bisected it and crossed through. "Need to make a table someday as well," he muttered.

"But where would you put it?" Hedd asked. "You need more space."

"Yes, we do. And you know what you'd better do?" Jack hollered over his shoulder as he strode toward his carpentry shop. "You'd better claim a plate and fill it 'cause I can't make more of them."

"Oh, I'm sure you could," Hedd yelled back. "I've seen ones made of wood."

"Stop jawing and start eating," Jack ordered with a surprising amount of humor in his voice. Not everyone took to her brothers' teasing so well. "Or there may be no food left for you when Max and Gus get here—which should be soon."

Robyn stared at the door, now equally dreading and anticipating it opening. Hedd had reacted unexpectedly to her new appearance. What would Max say, and do, when he saw her? And also saw Hedd in Noelle?

She hoped knowing two of her brothers still remained in Denver looking after Max's office was enough to keep him in Noelle. Until he saw her differently. Maybe tonight, her changes would inspire him enough to hold her hand or even kiss her.

CHAPTER 9

December 23, 1877
Two days until Christmas and the party

"He did nothing?" Felicity's voice rose with disbelief. For someone of average height, midway between Robyn and Birdie's stature, the reverend's wife had a very unaverage voice. She talked fast and had opinions on everything.

Usually Robyn appreciated such outspokenness, but discussing her challenges with Max had her squirming on her chair. "He said nothing about my hair, but he *did* ask me to work with him and Jack today."

She scanned the faces of the five women seated with her around Peregrines' office counter. Jane Creary had been too busy to join them, but her sister, Rosalind, had assembled a diverse crew of teachers. And with Jack's creation of a stool for Heddwyn, there were enough seats for everyone.

"Good for you for saying no. You're a guest in Noelle." Penny's gray eyes flashed like lightning as she slapped the counter, behaving a lot like Gus when he wanted to make a point.

Birdie had written that Gus had given Penny and many of the Brides of Noelle considerable advice about relationships and life. Seeing the mayor's wife now doing the same made Robyn smile.

Minnie shifted on her seat, with good reason. She, like Birdie, was pregnant. "Since you can't stay long, your time here should be a holiday."

Holiday. There was that word again. Practicing ladylike conversations—or the art of idle chatter as they'd also labeled the endeavor—with her new friends felt like a lot more work than hauling freight.

She'd rather speak plainly, even if the discussion forced her to address her issues with Max. "I told him I was staying at Peregrines because I wanted to try running the postal office."

Rosalind, whose family ran the nearby boardinghouse, wasn't one to take a holiday either. She rose and started refilling their cups. "I thought you said you wanted to spend more time with Jack's brother."

"I do. But his lack of reaction to my hair made me as ornery as a mule." She stiffened in remembrance, then her spirits slumped. "Plus, I felt guilty for not helping Birdie yesterday."

They all glanced toward the carpentry shop. Birdie and Daphne had retreated behind its closed door to discuss their dress and hat pairings. Away from the other women's nattering. Who knew conversation lessons could be so repetitive?

Say it like this.
Not quite right. It's more like this.
You've almost got it, but try this.

Ugh. She'd asked for *this*, but she struggled with forced politeness. She couldn't understand half of the things her new friends were saying. She had to keep trying, though, because her conversations with Max kept growing increasingly difficult. Maybe today's lessons would help. She was now inclined to try anything to resurrect their easy banter.

"What happened after you said you wouldn't work with him?" Felicity asked, driving the conversation as usual.

"Gus told me the steps for receiving and distributing the post. Then he declared that he was going to bed. That his fingers were tired from"—Robyn bit back the word *knitting* —"a secret project."

"More leather tooling gifts?" Penny smiled as she contemplated Gus' tool rack on the wall.

"Maybe," Robyn said with a shrug. "But last night, the strangest part was Birdie being short of breath. And after dinner, she admitted she was tired and went to bed early. I've never known her to slow down, let alone stop."

"She does appear paler than usual." Pearl's voice was quiet but concerned. Of Robyn's five instructors, the sheriff's wife was the most soft-spoken. Most of the time. Robyn couldn't imagine surviving a life of prostitution or breaking free from it, as Pearl had, without being incredibly strong.

Robyn's grip on her cup tightened. Since Brynmor lost the sight in his eye and could've easily lost his life at the same time, she'd become increasingly worried about losing the people she loved. With her feet resting on her stool's foot ring, she couldn't stop her knees from bouncing up and down.

When Pearl patted her hand, she went completely still. In the best way possible. Maybe she was getting used to all this...softer stuff. She felt an urge to hug Pearl.

The woman's words kept her still. "Being pale doesn't

always mean poor health. With Birdie's raven-black hair and midnight-blue eyes, her skin has always seemed startlingly white in comparison." Pearl had an eye for details, an artist's eye. Not only had she created the beautiful drawings proudly displayed in the Peregrines' office, but she'd helped Birdie with sketches of dress designs.

"Mothers shouldn't have to work so hard." When Rosalind paused refilling their cups to frown at Minnie, Robyn knew she was talking about more than Birdie or even her own mother. Minnie was devoted to helping the Creary family and many others in town.

"Having the skills and opportunity to support ourselves is a blessing." Felicity's voice rose like she was addressing a crowd rather than a group of five. "Not all women are so lucky. But, yes, juggling work and family life can be challenging."

Minnie caressed her rounded belly. "Has Birdie been sick to her stomach in the mornings?"

Robyn frowned. "Not that I've seen or heard."

"That's good. That part has been a challenge for me."

"It was kind of you to watch the postal office," Pearl said. "This way, if Birdie wants to take a nap, she can."

"She could even nap with her head here." Penny tapped the counter. "Like Grandpa Gus so often does."

"Is he with Birdie and Daphne?" Rosalind's gaze went to the carpentry shop.

"No, he's at Ezra's ranch. For the entire day."

"That will make it even easier for Birdie to relax." Penny released a wry chuckle. "Gus can be a handful to keep an eye on."

"What happened *after* Birdie went upstairs to bed? Did you get to talk to Max then?" Felicity's determination to hear everything about Robyn and Max remained strong.

"Jack said he had work to do behind the barn. Max, who'd been casting dark looks at my brother for leaving Denver, volunteered himself and Heddwyn to go with Jack and help him."

Pearl patted her hand again. "And you didn't go with them because you were still worried about Birdie and didn't want to leave her alone in the house with only Gus."

She'd become the worst handwringing saddle-goose imaginable. She needed to grab this conversation by the horns and turn it like she'd observed Felicity do today. "I wonder what Jack's working on? When I arrived and stabled my mount, I saw nothing but trees behind the Peregrines' barn."

"The view's no different from our boardinghouse." Rosalind filled the last cup, returned the kettle to the stove, and resumed her seat. "There's only that row of thick spruce and tall pines."

"Why hasn't Jack cut them down for his carpentry?" Robyn asked.

Penny's eyes shone with pride. "Charlie said the town founders chose to leave certain trees as windbreaks against the storms."

Penny's husband was a progressive-minded leader. From the stories Robyn had heard, she knew he was the best man to be mayor, even if some in town said differently.

"And there's nothing beyond those trees but snow." Minnie shrugged. "At least, the last I saw or heard." She and her husband had recently moved to a new house high on the bluff. They probably had a view of the entire town.

"Enough about trees," Felicity said. "What about your dance lessons?"

The change in topic made her thoughts spin. Was this

part of her conversation training? She stifled her groan. "I've tried twice, but Fina's been too busy both times."

"That's why you helped Fina yesterday," Penny said.

"She's been so generous in offering me lessons, like you've all been, that I..." she trailed off when she saw her teachers nodding as if they already knew. "How did you know about my helping Fina? Or that I asked for dance lessons?"

Rosalind winked at her. "Talk spreads fast in small towns."

And between families and friends who weren't keeping secrets. After Robyn met Jane at the diner yesterday, Jane must have told Rosalind, and Rosalind had told everyone in this room.

Robyn snorted a laugh, then apologized for the unlady-like sound. "Noelle's different from what I'm used to. My brothers and I have always lived in cities."

"It's an admirable accomplishment," Pearl said. "How your brothers raised you when they were no more than children themselves."

"Enough about the past. Let's look to the future." Felicity jumped to her feet. "Ladies, shall we proceed to the next step?"

Pearl's hand covered hers. Robyn couldn't resist her gentle tug. She left her seat and moved to Pearl's side of the counter.

Pearl kept pulling her forward. "We're taking to you see Fina."

She dug in her heels. "I can't leave."

Penny claimed Robyn's seat. "Gus also taught me the basics about the post."

Minnie moved her stool closer to Penny. "The two of us will handle this office while you're away."

Pearl and Rosalind linked arms with her and escorted her toward Felicity, who waited by the front door.

"While we three"—Felicity gestured to Pearl, Rosalind, and herself—"assist Nacho with his customers, so Fina has time to teach you dancing. We organized it all before we came here."

Their forethought and friendship overwhelmed and thrilled her. She was finally going to learn how to dance. If she mastered the activity, she stood a better chance of impressing Max at the Christmas party and—

Behind her, a loud screech made her whip around. Daphne stood in the carpentry shop's doorway. Her eyes were wide and panic-stricken.

Dread obliterated Robyn's happy hopes.

"Birdie's—" Daphne gasped, and her voice rose with incredulity. "Collapsed."

Robyn raced toward her.

"Minnie, stay here and help them. The rest of you, come with me." Felicity's orders bounced off the walls behind Robyn. "We must find Doctor Deane."

Daphne stumbled back inside the shop. Robyn followed her, nearly stepping on her heels. To where Birdie lay on the floor. Eyes closed. Face white as death.

She fell to her knees beside her. Tears stung her eyes. She couldn't see or breathe. She fumbled to find Birdie's hand. When she did, she clutched her limp fingers like they were a lifeline.

Birdie suddenly clasped her hand tight. "What am I doing on the floor?"

"You said you were tired and then you—" Daphne's voice broke.

"You finally lay down for a nap," Robyn teased, praying that was all that had happened.

When she swiped the tears from her eyes, she saw Daphne nodding in agreement, or at least in hope. The milliner's lips formed a determined line as she grabbed a roll of fabric and placed it gently beneath Birdie's head.

Her actions prompted Robyn to ask, "Are you cold or thirsty? Can we get you a blanket or some water?"

"Can you get—?" Despite the evenness in Birdie's voice, her hand shook in Robyn's grasp. "Jack"

What if she worsened while she was gone? What if this was their last moment together? Daphne could go. Her gaze went to her.

Daphne opened her mouth, then closed it quick, still struggling to speak.

It was up to her.

"I'll find him," Robyn vowed. She bolted out the back door toward the barn. Caradoc could carry her more swiftly around town. To wherever Jack was hauling freight. Or even to Ezra's ranch if Jack had gone early to pick up Gus.

Her ragged breathing muffled the crunch of her footsteps striking the packed snow path. Her blood pounded in her temples and ears. Her hands slipped on the barn door as she tried to yank it open. The fumble halted her long enough to hear the hammering in the air.

The beat called to her with a reassuring familiarity. She froze as she strove to pinpoint its source. Somewhere beyond the barn, where there was only a row of evergreen trees, where last night Jack had said he was going to work.

She leapt off the path and battled her way through the deep, unbroken snow. She silently cursed it, and her dress, for slowing her progress. Every breath had become essential to keep her legs moving. Her lungs burned with each stride.

When she reached the back of the barn, she glimpsed another trodden path. It led from the rear door straight to the trees. If she'd seen that door when she'd been inside the barn with Gus, she'd have known to go through the barn not around it.

She'd lost valuable time. Birdie was counting on her speedy return with Jack. She kept moving. She couldn't hear the hammering above her labored breathing. It might have halted, but she wouldn't.

Only when she gained the path did she glimpse the tunnel through the trees ahead. The shadowy arch pulled her like a beacon. The sweet scent of spruce and freshly cut wood enveloped her. The trimmed branches barely brushed her as she raced through their shade.

She burst into the light. Her feet and gaze climbed the rise of snow, up the trodden path to a house. With no door or windows. With a lot of other missing pieces. With no people in sight.

She sucked in a breath and screamed as loud as she could, "Jack!" Her voice wasn't strong enough. Her feet weren't fast enough. Birdie needed help, and she needed—"Max!"

He barreled out of the house, dropped the hammer in his hand, and pulled her into his arms. She clutched him close and never wanted to let go.

"What's wrong?" His voice rasped near her ear.

"Birdie."

Footsteps pounded down the path behind her. She glanced over her shoulder. Jack sprinted through the trees, racing toward the office.

Someone clasped her arm as tightly as she was holding Max. She looked up into Heddwyn's eyes, blue as the sky above him. She'd never been so happy that he hadn't kept his word, that he hadn't caught the train and returned to Denver.

He swallowed hard. "Is it her baby?"

She felt his fear. Shared it. Their mother had died after giving birth to her. "I don't know." All her worries about losing someone came to a head. She crumpled to her knees.

Max knelt with her. His hands cupped her cheeks and guided her gaze to meet his. "Whatever happens, we can face it together." He'd lost family as well. In the war, he'd dug for hours trying to save his father and brother. He'd only saved Jack. "We're going to help Birdie *and* Jack."

His resolve strengthened her. He must have sensed the change in her because he immediately stood and reached down to her. She seized his hand and scrambled to her feet. His unwavering grasp kept her upright. He didn't let go.

He held her hand all the way back to the office.

CHAPTER 10

*M*ax sat close to Robyn, her hand held firmly in his. He hadn't been able to let go since they returned to the office and clustered around Jack, who'd clutched Birdie's hands. While Birdie lay on the carpentry shop floor, murmuring reassurances to her husband and everyone. His tiny sister-in-law's steadfast bravery humbled him.

When Doctor Deane had arrived and instructed Jack to carry Birdie up to her bedroom, they'd followed them to the foot of the stairs and taken up this vigil, sitting on the closest workbench.

Everything upstairs remained silent. He glanced at Robyn. Her focus didn't waver from the staircase, but Heddwyn's gaze met his and seemed to ask the question he couldn't stop thinking.

What should we do next?

It was only the three of them now. Robyn kept them together. She held not only his hand but her brother's.

The Noelle ladies, who'd earned his eternal gratitude for their assistance today, had gone home. And he'd closed

Peregrines' Post. Locked the front door. A first, for this early in the day. The office didn't matter. What mattered were the people in it and, as he'd grown to realize, in Noelle as well.

This town was an exceptional one.

Behind Heddwyn, a blur of movement outside the carpentry shop's window snared his attention. The silhouette of a big man walking fast. The back door, which they hadn't locked, opened just as fast.

Their visitor hadn't bothered to knock because he'd also heard the stories about not needing to. Robyn's youngest brother, and the largest, filled the doorway.

"What's wrong?" Griffin demanded. "Why is your front door locked?"

Robyn released his hand, and Hedd's too, and ran to Griff. She threw her arms around him and hugged him tight.

Griff shot Hedd and Max a worried look as he patted his sister's back awkwardly, but his words flowed easily. "I missed you as well, Little Red."

Footsteps echoed in the hall upstairs. The doctor descended the steps.

Max and Hedd rose from their seats. Their voices joined Robyn's as they asked, "Is she—?"

"She's going to be fine," Doctor Deane interrupted.

A round of cheers went up. Robyn hugged the doctor, which made him smile. He'd probably seen it all in his line of work.

"However..." Deane set his medical bag on a bench and rubbed his eyes wearily. "Birdie still needs a lot of rest."

"We shouldn't have been so loud." Hedd froze as if he were afraid he'd step on a squeaky floorboard.

"We weren't thinking," Robyn whispered.

"We're sorry we—"

The doctor cut him off again. "No need to apologize. Birdie wasn't asleep when I left her, but I hope she will be soon. I've prescribed complete bed rest for several days. Maybe more."

Max released a lengthy sigh, relieved there was a way for Birdie to get better while unsure of its chances of success. "That'll be difficult for her."

Deane's gaze went to the second floor. "Jack seems to have a plan. He told Birdie that they could work on some secret project. When I objected, he assured me it was only handwork that could be done in bed. He said he couldn't say more."

"It's one of Gus' surprises." Max turned toward the door and the barn beyond. "I'd better hitch a team and get him from Ezra's ranch."

"That's being done for you," the doctor said. "After Felicity found me, she said her next task was getting your grandfather home."

The reverend's wife's foresight and generosity left Max at a loss for words.

When Robyn looped her arm around his, he was even more speechless.

She touched him so easily, like they stood this way every day. This, however, was another first. He stared at her like he'd been deprived of her presence for months. Seeing her long braid again brightened his mood. Not that he'd been unhappy seeing her with a different hairstyle yesterday. He was just happy to see her, no matter how she looked.

"Wait a minute." Doctor Deane's eyebrows arched as if he'd realized something. He was also pondering Robyn. "My wife met you yesterday at Avis and Liam's store. You're Miss Llewellyn. And you and Max are—"

"We work together in Denver." Robyn's arm tightened

around his like she worried he might run away. "Please call me Robyn, and when you see Felicity, thank her for us."

Us. The word was also new, but felt incredibly right.

"We thank you as well, Doctor." Max held out his hand.

Deane's handshake was as vigorous as Liam's and Culver's. "Glad to be of assistance and have you back in Noelle." His smile widened as his gaze went from Max to Robyn and kept moving. "Also, glad to find that neither of you is alone. You must be Robyn's brothers. And who might you be, miss?"

A slender woman, with eyes as dark as the obsidian hair hanging straight to her waist, stood by the door. When had she arrived?

Griff cleared his throat. "She came with me."

And they hadn't noticed her in the shadow of his bulk or later when they'd been focused on the doctor's news.

"Lark." Robyn's voice was sharp with accusation.

Hedd's usually flippant or flighty tone was firm. "Why is she here?"

They appeared to know the woman well, but he'd never heard them speak of her. What else hadn't Robyn shared with him? First coming to Noelle. Now this.

If she'd hidden things from him in Denver, where he'd thought they'd discussed everything, how could he ever hope she'd share her life with him after they left Noelle?

"Remember—" Doctor Deane reclaimed his bag and edged toward the door. "No loud conversations down here if you want Birdie to rest uninterrupted upstairs." He left before they could comment.

Griff crossed his arms as he muttered, "I had to get her out of Denver before Bryn saw her in trouble again."

Robyn glared at the woman who still didn't react in any

way. "Before she caused him to be permanently injured defending her again."

The forbidden subject. Brynmor's eye. Its familiarity should have brought relief, but hearing them speak so openly about it discombobulated him.

Robyn's words did a helluva lot worse to the woman who'd previously seemed carved of wood. The color drained from her tawny skin.

"Will Brynmor follow you to Noelle?" He regretted his question immediately.

The woman's expression turned hopeful, then horrified.

"Don't worry." Hedd faced Max, but the dart of his eyes toward Lark revealed he was reassuring both of them. Hedd couldn't stay angry with anyone for long. "Bryn won't leave your office unattended."

"What did you tell him before you left?" Robyn asked.

"I didn't—" Griff huffed and stared at the floor. "I'm an idiot."

Hedd started pacing the room. "There's never enough time for talk."

Maybe in Griff's rush to get Lark out of Denver, but not in Heddwyn's race to find an adventure in Noelle.

"Don't worry." Robyn repeated Hedd's words, but she looked only at Max. "You've enough worries here in Noelle without us adding to them. My brothers will fix the mess they made. They'll board the first train to Denver tomorrow."

Griff stood tall again. "We'll work double-time to catch up your freight runs."

Hedd's fist pumped the air. "We'll drive faster than we ever have!"

"Shh." Robyn pressed her finger to her lips. She pulled Max out of the carpentry shop and into the office.

Everyone followed them, and Griff carefully closed the door.

"Right," Hedd mumbled. "Birdie must sleep, and we must go to Denver. It's the only thing to do."

"Actually, it isn't." Max groaned, having trouble believing what he was about to say. But say it he must. "I'd rather you stayed here."

Robyn's brothers gaped at him like he'd gone crazy.

"Just for one day, then you must return to Denver and Brynmor." He placed his palm over Robyn's hand still griping his arm, not wanting her to go anywhere. "We don't want him to be alone on Christmas Day."

"What would we do in Noelle?" Griff asked.

"*Just for one day*?" Hedd added.

Robyn leaned against him. "Make a new home."

He smiled at her head almost resting on his chest. She still knew him well, even if he worried he didn't always understand her so well.

"If Jack won't be leaving Birdie's bedside, he needs—" He shifted closer to Robyn. "I need more hands to finish the house he was building for her."

"I'll help." Lark spoke swiftly in a rasping but lyrical tone that made Max think she'd be a fine singer. What impressed him most, however, was that her first words were so selfless.

"What happened to your voice?" Robyn demanded.

Lark's shoulders lifted in the smallest of shrugs. "Life."

"Thank you," Robyn said grudgingly. "For offering to help us. *This time*."

"Any help is appreciated," Max reminded her.

When Robyn didn't reply, and neither did her brothers, he strove to say something that might break or at least lighten the tension. "And any friend of the Llewellyns is always welcome to stay with the Peregrines."

"She's not—" Robyn's glower disappeared when she glanced up at him. Uncertainty flashed in her eyes before she dropped her gaze. "Always friendly. You'll see."

"I can't afford to be," Lark whispered as if her words pained her. "And I can't stay here long. I also have people I need to help."

"She came looking for them in Denver." Griff claimed a seat by the counter and gestured for Lark to do the same.

Robyn sighed. "You did the right thing bringing her here. Together we can—" She inhaled sharply and for the first time looked at Lark with sympathy. "I'm sorry you won't be spending your Christmas with your family."

Lark slumped on her chair. Just as quickly, she raised her chin and changed the subject. "You mentioned a house. When do you wish it done?"

Max's hopes weren't realistic, but he voiced them anyway. "In a day."

"That's—" Hedd waved his hands in the air as if he'd find the end of his sentence there.

Griff propped his elbow on the counter and his chin on his palm as he contemplated his brother. "I take it there's still a fair bit to do?"

"We completed the siding today, but the house needs some flooring, doors, and windows, which are stacked in the back of the barn." Max frowned. "I've probably forgotten more that must be done."

"You've *forgotten* about this morning's freight not getting hauled. You've *forgotten* how to—" Hedd paced the freight aisle.

"Be you." Despite his swift assessment, Griff looked confounded.

Hedd halted beside his brother. "And tomorrow, there'll be even more freight."

"And the post office will need minding again," Robyn reminded them.

"So, it's impossible?" Lark asked.

"No." Robyn and her two brothers spoke as one, then grinned at each other.

Max had watched them and Brynmor do this many times. They thrived on talking about and then tackling challenges.

Robyn grabbed her brothers' hands. "We're family. If we stick together, we can do anything."

As she said the last word, her gaze met his. His disappointment that she wasn't holding his hand eased, but only a little. He'd have to get used to giving up her touch if he wanted to do what was best for her and everyone inside Peregrines' Post.

He had many gifts to organize.

A finished house for Jack and Birdie. A safe place for Lark until she was ready to move on. Enough time to get Hedd and Griff home to Bryn. And for Robyn... He knew what she wanted. There was one thing she'd talked about achieving in Noelle and hadn't yet accomplished. That would be his gift to her.

But he only had tonight and tomorrow to make it all happen. And then it'd be the 25th. All of his plans had changed and essentially become one.

He was giving Robyn and her family, and his as well, the best Christmas possible.

CHAPTER 11

December 24, 1877
One day until Christmas and the party

*T*he midday sun shone through the newly installed windows and into the two front rooms of Jack and Birdie's new house. Robyn struggled to keep her focus on the task at hand. And not on Max, striding up and down the hall and stairs—and in and out of her line of sight—as he greeted and thanked and organized the workers who kept coming to help with the construction.

There hadn't been much hope of finishing until they'd started arriving. The Noelle townsfolk were giving the Peregrines the best gift of all—their time.

She sanded the counter faster, resisting the temptation to linger over the beauty of how it matched the counter at Peregrines' Post in all the best ways while still being shaped to meet Birdie's specific needs.

Jack's newest creation would be the centerpiece of her new dress shop. And on the other side of the hall, visible through a pair of matching double doorways, would be

Jack's new carpentry shop. At first, Robyn had been dumb-founded by the perfection of the layout. Then she remembered Jack didn't have to guess what would make Birdie the happiest.

His desires matched his wife's. Being close to each other in work and in rest.

More than ever, Robyn wanted that closeness with Max. And as soon as she completed this task, she'd have an excuse to talk to him. For the briefest of moments. Then she'd receive her next job and rush to finish it so she could talk to him again. That had been her routine all day.

Her arms ached with fatigue and her stomach rumbled with hunger, but she wouldn't stop. Not when she was doing the most important work imaginable and when she'd be talking to Max in— She scanned the remaining counter that required sanding. In no more than five minutes. Her hands moved faster and her breath grew shorter, but her happiness remained steadfast.

Until Lark, who was sanding a cabinet in the same room and who hadn't said a word all day, murmured, "He's a good man."

The grief Brynmor had suffered because of Lark made Robyn growl like an overprotective mother bear. "So is my brother."

Lark flinched, dropped her sandpaper, retrieved it and went back to sanding. All without a word.

Robyn pressed her lips tight and silently cursed her temper and Lark for being so savvy or observant, or maybe both. They barely knew each other, and judging those you didn't know, or thought you knew, was unforgivable.

A sudden realization made her wince as well. That was her only problem with Lark. She couldn't forgive the woman for hurting her brother physically and emotionally.

He'd once called Lark a good friend. Had he thought of her as his best friend? She cursed herself again. Of course, he had. She now saw that Bryn had felt the same way about Lark as Robyn felt about Max.

And Lark? What did she feel? In the past, she'd often wondered if the usually calm and collected woman felt anything.

"I never meant for him to get hurt." Lark's voice grew even more raspy as she answered Robyn's unspoken question.

What had happened to her voice? It'd always been exceptionally smooth. Her singing had easily earned her many suitors until they learned why she had darker skin. Or accepted what they'd already guessed. Lark was half native. She came from a tribe up north. Or so the man who'd managed her singing troupe had said.

People often hated others for the most outrageous reasons. Robyn, along with Hedd and Griff, only disliked Lark for hurting Bryn.

In the silence that descended between them, the previously pleasant sound of sanding grated on Robyn's nerves.

As did Lark's next words. "You mentioned an injury. How bad is it?"

Bad enough to scar not only his body but his soul. But Bryn never wanted to talk about his eye.

Robyn didn't want to either, so she asked her own question. "What did you think would happen when you came looking for him?"

"Not him. My sisters. I didn't know he'd settled in Denver."

"You must miss them."

"Them and—" Lark gulped a breath as if her thoughts as well as her throat hurt her. "Brynmor, too."

Robyn's rebuff died on her lips. Somehow, she knew Lark wasn't lying. Her brother and Lark had formed an instantaneous bond when they first met. Unfortunately, that hadn't stopped Lark from siding with her sisters when their well-being clashed with Robyn's brother's. "I miss my brother as well."

"You'll be happy to return to Denver," Lark replied.

"Not to the city, but to Bryn, yes."

"Here in Noelle, you and the Peregrines are blessed with so many friends." Lark gestured toward the hallway. "More have come."

Josefina and an unknown woman with pretty copper-colored curls—and not blazing bright red like hers—stood in the doorway with their arms full of small packages.

Robyn rushed to them. "Fina, it's wonderful to see you again."

"And you too. We brought you nourishment." Fina tilted her head to her companion. "This is Victoria. She runs the bakery and sweet shop with her husband."

"I helped Fina make your sandwiches, and as we were wrapping them..." Victoria grinned wickedly. "I couldn't resist adding a treat for you and all of your helpers."

"Thank you." Robyn took the load from Victoria's arms. When Lark arrived at her side and silently transferred Fina's packages into her own arms, Robyn introduced her.

"It was kind of you to think of us," Robyn added. "What do Max and I owe you?"

Both Fina and Victoria shook their heads and said, "Nothing."

Lark gasped. "But you've brought so much."

Victoria's smile didn't waver as she addressed Lark. "This is our gift to Jack and Birdie for always doing *so much* for everyone in Noelle."

"And not only them. Robyn helped me at my diner yesterday. And Max..." Fina's eyes sparked with mischief as she winked at Robyn. "Well, I couldn't refuse him anything after he asked for your gift."

"*My* gift?"

"Yes, and I'm ready to give it." Fina set her hands on her hips and struck a theatrical pose. "Where is he?"

"Somewhere in this house." Her heart raced with excitement. She now had an immediate excuse to find Max and talk to him. "Let's put the food in the kitchen and look for him."

She led the way to the back room. To a kitchen with the longest table she'd ever seen and six chairs made to match the number but not the height of the stools currently in Peregrines' Post. And best of all, to Max who stood in the kitchen placing dishes in a cupboard.

A domestic task that made her grin.

Max took pride in completing any type of work, whether it was organizing an entire town to finish his brother's house, or four Llewellyn teamsters to run a Denver freight office, or simply knitting the woolen cap that she wore right now.

He couldn't give her a better gift.

Except for maybe a lifetime of his smiles.

When he smiled back at her, she sped up her pace, eager to reach him. And caught her skirt on the corner of the table. And stumbled. And could only curse as the weight of the packages in her arms made her tumble straight toward the floor.

Before she could drop her cargo and brace herself for her fall, Max caught her in his arms. Her shock quickly turned to delight at having him hold her—even if the food nestled between them formed a barrier. Maybe she should trip more often. But that would be dishonest. But she wanted Max to hold her like this. But she wanted him to do it eagerly and not merely to prevent her from hurting herself.

Max's eyes widened with amazement as he stared down at her.

She muttered another curse. "Sorry. I may never get the hang of this dress."

"Don't apologize. I was more fascinated by the expressions flashing across your face than by your falling. You're... mesmerizing."

She snorted. "What I am is a menace to myself, and others, when wearing this dress."

"Maybe you shouldn't wear it." His face went as red as his beard, but he didn't let go of her.

If she didn't wear Birdie's beautiful creation, what could she possibly wear to impress him? Probably nothing. Or maybe...*actually* nothing? She felt her own face heat at the thought. "You never liked this dress."

He heaved a sigh. "I hate to say it, but I've always liked it. A lot."

"That's an odd thing to say. Confusing as well."

"Then let me be clear. And damn the consequences." He leaned so close that their noses touched and whispered, "I *like* seeing you in a dress as much as seeing you in trousers. My main *dislike* is not seeing enough of you lately."

"I think I should come back another time." Fina's words faded along with her footsteps down the hall.

Max lifted his head from hers. "No!"

The volume of his voice startled her.

"No more delays," he said less loudly but even more intensely. "I want you to have your gift right now. The *one thing* you wanted more than anything else."

"You."

He blinked in surprise. "Me?"

She pressed her lips tight. She was making a muddle of things again. He wanted to give her a gift, and she was acting like she didn't want it because she wanted him most of all. "What I meant to say was...*you* are kind to get me something. What is it?"

"Dance lessons."

"That's why Fina's here!" She glanced across the room to see if she was still there.

Fina stood by the hall doorway, grinning at them. "Max arranged everything. He even asked Felicity and the ladies who visited you yesterday to cover for me at the diner, so no one will interrupt your lessons. Not that someone from the diner would come all the way out here and do that, but..." She shrugged. "You never know."

Max's gift wasn't only dance lessons but his time to arrange them. And hadn't she been thinking that giving your time was the best gift of all?

Her vision went blurry with tears. When she ducked her head to hide them, the food started falling from her arms. Max released her and bent to pick them up, while Fina and Victoria helped her and Lark get the rest of the packages onto the table without dropping any more.

"I love your gift," she blurted and stared out the window at the starkly white snow outside.

"Are you sure? Your brothers could—" He released another weary sigh. "Well, maybe it was just Griffin. They jabbered about a lot of things in my office the day you left."

She'd asked them to tell Max she'd gone to Noelle. They, however, often got off-track and said a lot more. Right now, there was only one thing left to say. She spun to face him. "I'll need a dance partner."

"You'll find plenty of 'em at the Christmas party tomorrow." Gus rubbed his hands together as he rushed from the hall to the table.

Max scowled at his grandfather, but when his gaze shifted to her, he straightened his shoulders and said, "Grandpa's right."

"Of course, I am."

No! I don't want you to be right. I want to dance with Max.

"I got a nose fer sniffin' out the truth. And sandwiches too." He claimed one and groaned happily after the first bite. "I could smell 'em all the way upstairs. You better eat fast," he told Robyn between mouthfuls. "Noelle's bachelors are gonna keep you busy. I heard three—who are at the top of my matchmaking list—pacing circles outside the front door while they argued about you. Although it'll do you no good dancing with any of them since they're yer brothers."

Robyn's stomach lurched. "What are Hedd and Griff doing outside? They promised to board a train to Denver as soon as they finished the last Noelle freight run."

Max grabbed her hand. The solid warmth of his big fingers around hers elated her until she saw him frowning at Lark.

"He said three." Max's gaze cut to her, and his frown deepened. "Your *three* brothers."

Her stomach plummeted.

"Of course, I did." Gus huffed. "I ain't so old or so hungry that I've lost the ability to count."

In the brittle silence that followed, the squeak of the new door opening and slamming at the other end of the hall echoed like gunfire. The thump of heavy boots approached. Then halted. Abruptly.

"Stop jumpin' in front of me." Bryn's growl was unusually menacing.

"We would if you'd be reasonable," Griff hissed back.

"Yeah, *stop* being so ornery," Hedd complained. "Agree to return to the train depot and we can—"

A tussle erupted.

"Go," Max whispered and pushed her toward Lark.

"I ain't leavin' till I get answers." Brynmor's voice thundered down the hallway. So did footsteps.

Robyn yanked Lark toward the back door, which Max had opened to speed their escape. She leapt out with Lark in tow.

"First, Rob abandons me. Next, you two knuckleheads." Still in the hallway, Bryn's accusation held more loneliness than anger. He'd never been without them. He'd gone from brother to father. He'd shaped his whole life around them.

Only a puff of air marked the blessedly silent closing of the door behind her. She staggered through the snow, fighting her skirt and her guilt for leaving Bryn again.

Inside the kitchen, his raised voice was muffled, but she still caught every word. "At least Rob told me where she was going. She wouldn't—"

Silence descended around her. Not even a bird chirped or a tree branch rustled. She glanced over her shoulder.

Bryn stood in the center of the kitchen, gaping at her and Lark through the window.

She wouldn't desert me completely. He didn't say the words, but she heard them nonetheless ringing in her head.

He'd caught her abandoning him. Caught Lark as well. Again.

He yanked open the door, then just as quickly turned his back to them. "Help your sister and—" He paced the room, waving his hands wildly like Hedd often did. "Just get them out of the snow and the cold."

Hedd and Griff scrambled to comply. Max beat them to

it. He thrust his hand out to her. She pulled Lark—who stood surprisingly tall and undaunted beside her—forward and put Lark's hand in Max's. When Lark was back inside, Hedd and Griff jostled each other to reach past Max and help Robyn in as well.

Max elbowed them aside and seized her hand. He didn't let go. Not even when he moved to close the door behind her.

"Well, ain't this a fine sight to see." Gus was the only one smiling in the room. "All of the Llewellyns finally in Noelle. Business must be slow in Denver for you to be here."

Robyn's guilt grew. Her family had let Max down.

"I'll come back later. Tonight. Or tomorrow morning." Fina gave Max an apologetic look as she edged toward the hallway with Victoria close beside her. "There's still time."

Robyn's shoulders slumped. Her family had also ruined the gift Max had invested so much time organizing for her.

Max's fingers tightened around hers. "Fina, I know it's not a good time, but if you stayed, I believe it'd help. Brynmor needs to talk to his sister, and Robyn needs to learn how to dance. They can do that together."

No! She stifled the selfish word. She wanted to dance with Max, but she couldn't do that. She must do what was best for everyone else in this room.

"Where shall we do the lessons?" Fina asked.

"In Jack's new carpentry room." Max thrust his chin toward the front of the house. "It's the only one without any furniture yet. My brother listed everything else as a higher priority."

"I'll meet you there," Fina said as she slipped out of the kitchen with Victoria.

Still keeping a hold on her hand, Max thrust sandwiches

into Hedd's and Griff's hands. "Go see if there's anything that needs finishing in Birdie's dress shop room."

The one across from the carpentry shop where Bryn would be. Max was making sure her brothers stayed near Bryn. Just in case.

Her brothers glanced worriedly at her.

"Better hurry up," she urged. "There's lots of sanding to finish." There wasn't, but she hoped adding to the size of the task would finally get them moving.

When they left, Max turned to Gus. "Grandpa—"

"Yeah, yeah. Get upstairs 'n get back to work. Yer about as much fun as Jack when he's snapping the reins."

Max gestured to the sandwiches on the table. "Can you take some food upstairs for our helpers? Better grab a second sandwich for yourself."

"Now yer talkin' my language, Maximilian Boy!"

When Gus had left with his arms overflowing with food, Max said to Lark, "You should sit down and also try to eat something."

Max was right. Although Lark still stood tall and faced Bryn head on, her skin had resumed the pallor from when she'd arrived and first heard about his injury.

"Mor," she whispered in a raspier voice than ever before.

Lark flinched along with Bryn. Her being the only one to use this special nickname, that should've been so obvious to Robyn and her brothers, showed how connected she was to Bryn. Or had been.

"I'm sorry," Lark whispered. "I never meant for—"

"No." He spun sideways and stared at the wall, keeping his clouded eye as far from Lark as possible. He'd never hidden his injury from anyone before. "I don't want your pity. I only want to know why you left me in Cheyenne."

The starch went out of Lark's spine. She sat down on the nearest chair.

"Brynmor—"

"What?" Bryn barked, cutting off Max.

"Lark will be here when you're done helping Robyn learn how to dance and when you've *hopefully*"—he stressed the word like a warning, not a hope—"calmed down."

Bryn glared at him.

"I promise she's not going anywhere," Max vowed. "You can trust me."

Bryn threw his hands in the air. "Fine. I'll do as you suggest." His gaze jumped from Max to Lark to Robyn, then back to Max. "*You've* never given me a reason not to believe your words."

Remorse twisted Robyn's stomach into a knot as he retreated down the hall and away from her.

Max pressed two sandwiches into her palms and cupped her hands in his, still not letting go. A sudden wave of fatigue made her unbearably tired. He'd be letting go very soon. He had to.

"Take these and try to get him to eat something with you." A wry smile tugged his lips then disappeared. "I think I'm turning into my brother with all my bossy fussing."

"Whatever you do is perfect. Thank you for always helping me with my brothers."

"They need you. Especially Brynmor. And I want you to have your lessons. You can distract him with them and who knows..." He smiled again, but his eyes remained dark with uncertainty. "Learning to dance might one day help him win the heart of the woman he loves."

And Max? What would he do when he fell in love and wanted to dance with that lucky lady?

She wished he loved her and needed her and— Guilt

swamped her again. Max did need her. Just not in the way she'd hoped for and schemed to achieve. He needed his friend back.

He needed her to get her brothers back on track. Back to Denver to help run his office. Where she would go as well. To make sure they all did their jobs.

But first she must help him finish Birdie and Jack's house.

She opened her mouth to say she didn't need dance lessons, but then closed it. This was his gift to her. And she wouldn't deny him the chance to give something if that was what would make him happy.

She flung her arms around his neck and hugged him close. Her voice cracked as she said, "I'm so sorry things didn't work out between us. But I'll treasure your friendship forever."

She released him before he could answer or see the tears flooding her eyes again. She bottled up her unhappiness, pressed it deep down in a corner of her heart, and raced from the room.

CHAPTER 12

December 25, 1877
The morning of the Christmas party

esterday, he'd held Robyn in his arms. Twice. And he'd let her go twice. First, so she could begin her dance lessons with him as her partner. Second, so she could have those same lessons with her brother instead.

Because he'd seen it in her eyes and felt it in their embrace. She'd been willing to give up the thing she'd told her brothers she most wanted and had been struggling for days to achieve in Noelle. She'd give up her happiness rather than let Brynmor say something he'd regret if left alone with Lark.

That was yesterday. Today, they couldn't stop Bryn from doing something rash every moment that he and Lark remained in Noelle. Together, but now no longer talking. As far as he knew, the pair hadn't said a word to each other since their reunion in the new house.

Never had one of Griffin's favorite sayings summed them up so well.

We're all idiots.

Why couldn't he have let go of his determination to help Robyn with her worries about Bryn? *Then I'd have danced with her. And I'd be happy.*

He shook his head. He couldn't be happy if Robyn wasn't happy.

A glum-looking Robyn worked beside him as they loaded the last of Jack's tools and wooden legs into two burlap sacks. She didn't speak, or smile, or even meet his gaze. She just worked.

She hadn't stopped since her dance lesson finished and she'd resumed helping with Jack and Birdie's house. He'd had to escort her off the worksite before she'd sleep. At least during that all too short walk, he'd got to hold her hand again.

But she hadn't smiled. Not then and not now.

Maybe it was because she was exhausted. They all were. Her brothers were with Gus and Lark, doing final preparations at the house. And Peregrines' Post and Freight was once again closed for the day. In both Noelle and Denver.

"I'm sorry my brothers left your office unattended." Robyn's tone was an odd combination of angry and remorseful.

She was startlingly good at guessing what he was thinking, while not quite understanding his thoughts. She'd apologized many times yesterday for her brothers' leaving Denver, but this was the first time today.

"Don't worry about it," he said firmly. "It's Christmas Day. And today, whatever is happening, or not happening, in Denver doesn't seem that important."

The floorboards creaked upstairs. They hurried to pack the final items as a single pair of footsteps echoed down the hall towards them. They hid their sacks behind them before straightening as one to face the stairs and Jack descending with Birdie in his arms.

A vigorous rustling close beside him snapped his gaze back to Robyn. She swiped at the dust streaking her skirt. A disapproving scowl etched her brow. She didn't do things half-measure. He'd always admired her for that. But her attachment to the dress confused the heck out of him.

Robyn might say and act like she disliked wearing the garment, but she still wore it. Probably for Birdie, who'd made the outfit with care and affection but couldn't see what Robyn wore right now.

Birdie sneezed and rubbed her nose below the blindfold covering her eyes.

"Are you catching a chill?" Jack asked worriedly.

"No, I'm—"

"Trying to steal a peek?"

"No," Birdie said, laughing. "I'm *trying* to survive the dust. Is this part of the surprise?" She sniffed the air. "Your shop smells different."

"That's because—" Jack's jaw dropped as he surveyed the empty room.

Their early morning scramble to remove everything had raised a haze.

"Because what?" Birdie demanded.

"He can't say," Max answered. "The dust is part of the surprise."

"We wanted Christmas surprises for both of you," Robyn added.

Late last night, when they'd met Jack in this room to

relay a report on the house, the shop had been full. Jack had told them not to worry about moving anything here. That he'd deal with it later. He'd thanked them profusely for all their hard work and urged them to get some sleep.

After Jack had gone back to Birdie, they'd both agreed they wanted their work to be as complete as possible. So, transporting this room's contents had become their morning task. That and one item from upstairs. They hadn't dared do more and make a noise in the hall that might give away their surprise.

"Merry Christmas," Robyn said at the same time as he did.

Which made him smile. And finally, she smiled with him. When she did, the fatigue etching her face eased. He prayed the tension between them would wane as well.

"And a Merry Christmas to the two of you." Birdie's grin turned into a pout. "But is carrying me wherever we're headed really necessary?"

"Doc Deane said complete bed rest. So, it's either a mattress or my arms." Jack pressed a lingering kiss to the top of his wife's raven-haired head. "Besides, you're carrying two very important packages right now, so it's only right that I carry you."

Birdie laughed, and her hand went from the bundle wrapped in red cloth she held to her rounded belly.

Max opened the door for them to go out. Then he grabbed his own bundle, waited for Robyn to retrieve hers, and closed the door behind them. With his sack slung over his shoulder like Saint Nicholas, he followed Robyn, who followed Jack.

Jack barely limped as they walked single file down a path tramped in the snow by the many helpers who'd come and gone this way yesterday. *Bless them and the entire town.*

They'd helped transform Jack's dream gift for Birdie into a fully formed reality.

When their group came through the trees, his gaze raced up the footpath to the house. As always, the structure's perfect symmetry framing the front door called to him like a warm welcome to enter. If one could resist the wide, covered porch that promised as many pleasant moments outside as might be found inside.

A familiar, thin but wiry figure rose from his seat on the steps. Grandpa Gus shoved a lumpy object under his coat. When he rushed forward to stand in front of Jack, who'd halted with Robyn and Max beside him, the tips of a pair of knitting needles protruded from their hiding place. Same as they had the morning after Max arrived in Noelle. After Gus had found Max's abandoned needles in Peregrines' Post.

"Why have we stopped?" Birdie asked.

At a nod from Jack, Gus removed her blindfold and stepped back with a grand sweep of his arm to reveal the house as he hollered, "Surprise! We made something for you."

"You made me a..." Tears spilled from Birdie's eyes. "*Un nid.*"

Robyn's alarmed gaze searched his. "What's a nid?"

He shrugged. He hadn't a clue.

"A *nid* is a nest. *Une maison et une—*" Birdie shrugged as well and laughed. "*Maison.* A house and a home are the same word in French, but sometimes so different in life."

"So...you like it?" Jack asked.

"*Oui!* But like is too little a word. Your gift is *incroyable et fantastique et—*" She paused only to draw in a quick breath before saying on a sigh, "Absolutely perfect."

"It will be soon." Jack cradled her closer. "I'm going to make everything better."

"You always do. *Merci.*" Birdie kissed his cheek, then looked at Gus, then Robyn and Max. "Thank you all very much."

"Let's get you inside and out of the cold." Jack hurried up the steps.

Birdie craned her neck to see the porch above and around her. "When did you have time to create all of this?"

Jack slipped through the open doorway. "I built the foundation months ago. Then the bridge was blown up, the railroad was delayed, and I was swamped with freight runs. Only since the track's completion and folks now using it for shipments, have I had time to work here again."

"It must've been difficult to keep this large a secret," Birdie murmured.

"He didn't even tell me," Gus grumbled.

"I wanted it to be a surprise." When Jack carried Birdie into her dress shop room, their group parted ways to give them some privacy.

Gus disappeared down the hall toward the kitchen while Max and Robyn took their sacks into Jack's carpentry room.

As they unloaded the last items, Birdie's delighted but muffled words grew loud with amazement. "*C'est pas possible!* Your shop is across the hall? That's beyond perfect."

"That's what I thought," Robyn whispered so softly he almost didn't hear her.

Jack came into the room, still carrying Birdie. His expression became as astounded as his wife's. "You not only moved my shop, but you set it up?"

Max leaned back against a workbench and surveyed the room. "Most likely we put everything in the wrong place. It'll take some effort to reorganize."

"But it's work I can tackle at home with Birdie near. Thanks to you."

"It's the least I could do after being away for so long." He raked his fingers through his hair. Its tangled mess felt a lot like Jack's hair always looked. He'd left Noelle because he wanted to be his own man. And he'd done that. He'd changed. But now? How could he, after only a few days back in Noelle, be starting to not only act but look like his brother again?

"Well, you're here now." Birdie said. "And that's the best gift of all."

"Yes, but I still need to ask if he'll—" Birdie's elbow in Jack's ribs halted him.

"It's Christmas," she said. "That discussion can wait until all of the gifts are given."

Max gestured down the hall. "There's more waiting for you in the kitchen."

Jack raised his chin as he inhaled deeply. "I can smell the feast from here."

The delicious scents made Max stand tall as well.

Once again, Jack led the way. "How did you find time to cook, move Birdie's shop and mine, and finish the house?"

"My brother, Brynmor, did the cooking." Robyn's voice suddenly sounded twice as tired as before. She trudged like a crusader who'd walked too long and too far and doubted her destination or what she'd previously held sacred. "Just as he's always done wherever we've lived or set up camp."

She'd told him many times how relieved she and her brothers had been to settle in Denver, to have a home no matter how humble, to not have to move again. She'd left all of that to come here...and so had her brothers.

"I didn't make today's meal on my own," Bryn muttered as he placed a steaming pot of cawl soup on the table. He strode back to the stove for the roast lamb. "I had help."

Gus licked his lips and hovered close to the bounty. "Turns out Lark is Brynmor's match in the kitchen."

Bryn didn't say more, and Lark didn't say anything. They simply worked together, bringing the last of the dishes of cottage pie and sugared Welsh cakes to the table. Their actions reminded Max of his and Robyn's silently stiff partnership this morning, which had seemed to get even tenser as they'd taken the final steps to reach this kitchen.

When he circled the table so he could see her expression, he found her frowning at Heddwyn and Griffin.

Hedd scrubbed his hand over the back of his neck. "We tried to help."

"But it's hard to know how," Griff griped, "when people won't say much."

When Bryn shot them a quelling glare, his brothers folded their arms stubbornly but also defensively.

"All *we're saying*," Hedd muttered, "is that if anything's burnt, blame the master chef, not us."

"Everything smells and looks too delicious to be burnt." Jack smiled reassuringly at them. "Thank you all for this wonderful gift."

"Yes, and thank you, Lark," Birdie added, "for being here today. It's a pleasure to meet you."

"And you as well," Lark said quietly but without hesitation.

"We had better eat before the food gets cold." Gus recited a swift but heartfelt prayer of thanks, then thrust plates into Lark's and Bryn's hands and filled one for himself. "Cooks 'n old-timers should eat first."

"Why is there a bed by the table?" Birdie stared as if bewildered at the one item Robyn and Max had moved from Peregrines' Post's second floor this morning. The bed from Max's old room.

Before nightfall, they would hopefully have moved everything else from upstairs. Right now, everyone needed to eat, including Birdie, who could do so reclining on the bed in the kitchen. Jack had been insistent that she have the complete bed rest the doctor ordered.

"It's your throne, milady," Hedd said with a wink. "Now you really have the perfect perch to be...Hen Who Rules the Roost."

"I'll never get used to this pampering," Birdie replied. "This is too much."

"There's no such thing when we're together," Jack murmured close to her ear as he set her carefully on the bed. His hands lingered near her, arranging her pillows and blankets.

For the first time since he'd arrived in Noelle, Bryn's voice resumed its deeply protective and nurturing tone as he said, "Tell me what you like, Birdie, and I'll bring your food to you."

The Llewellyns visibly relaxed as their big brother's manner regained some normalcy. Hedd and Griff even started whistling a surprisingly harmonious Christmas carol. Relief made Max hum along.

They could all use a respite from their work and their worries. He'd let Robyn eat, then he'd...ask her to sit on the porch with him. That serene spot would be the best location for nurturing a conversation that might also get them back to normal. And if not, they could sit and say nothing. They'd at least be together.

He filled a plate for Jack, knowing what he liked, and gave it to his brother at the same time Bryn presented Birdie with her food.

When Jack held out his hand to Bryn, the Welsh giant shook it firmly.

"It's good to finally meet you, Big Hill." Without waiting for an answer, Jack peered around Bryn's broad bulk and called to Griff, "And you too, Ruddy."

Griff gave him a brisk salute. "Thanks for making us feel right at home, Busy Bee."

When Bryn shot his baby brother a questioning look, Griff thrust his chin at Hedd and went back to eating.

Hedd's chest puffed up proudly. "I came up with the name all on my own and only a few minutes after meeting him. Busy Bee was so impressed he made me a chair."

Jack frowned as his gaze swept the number of seats in the kitchen. "I should've made more for out here. I didn't plan this all that well."

There were only six chairs and nine of them. With Birdie on the bed and Jack now claiming a seat on the floor closest to her, they were short just one.

So, Max sat on the floor next to his brother and gestured for Gus and their guests to take the chairs. Which unfortunately resulted in Robyn sitting much too far away from him. He consoled himself by pondering his plan to talk to her on the porch before she went to the Christmas party.

He shook his head. No, that event was still a few hours away, and a lot could happen between now and then. Like, he hoped, her deciding not to go.

Birdie brushed her fingers through Jack's wild hair. "You can't plan for everything, my very Busy Bee."

"Truer words were never spoken." For the first time since they'd entered the kitchen, Bryn finally looked at his sister. "How have your Noelle plans been going, Rob?"

Her spoon hit her plate. She caught it before it struck the floor. She also caught herself in mid-curse and said in a primly polite voice, "Pardon me. What I meant to say was...if nothing else, my plans to learn to dance have been achieved.

Thanks to Max for organizing my lessons and Fina's expert instructions."

Robyn's stilted speech confounded Max until he remembered she'd undertaken conversation lessons with the Noelle women the day before yesterday. That might explain her formal language, but not the stiffness in its delivery.

Bryn's shoulders hunched. "I should've taught you long ago."

"Yes, you should have," Robyn replied briskly.

Griffin paused devouring a Welsh cake to ask, "How could he teach you something he doesn't know how to do?"

"He knows." Robyn's voice had grown colder than a storm circling a mountain.

"No, he doesn't. He's never—" Hedd's confident expression turned wary.

"What aren't you telling us, Rob?" Griff demanded.

"It's what Bryn hasn't been telling us." Her steely blue gaze shot daggers at her eldest brother. "Fina said you were an excellent dancer. Yesterday wasn't your first lesson, was it?"

Bryn hung his head. "Lark taught me in Cheyenne."

"So, you could've taught me *in Denver*," Robyn shot back. "But you didn't. Why?"

"I didn't want to..." he shrugged, "...remember how I learned."

"You'd rather keep secrets," Robyn muttered as she glowered at her plate.

"Apparently, we all would." Bryn's gaze darted in Lark's direction. He still wasn't talking to her, but he'd said something about her. And not unkindly. That was a start.

Unfortunately, it was also an end.

Bryn's revelation terminated not only the Llewellyns'

conversation but everyone's. They finished eating in silence. Then they washed their plates and put everything away.

The quiet helped Max rally his hopes and plans for Robyn. *Now is the time. Fortune favors the bold. He who hesitates is lost.* He shook his head. He was not only becoming more and more like his brother, but like Gus, who gave endless advice.

Stop rambling and ask her to talk to you out on the porch.

CHAPTER 13

*C*hagrin for being angry with Brynmor kept Robyn's gaze downcast. First on her plate, then on the many plates she helped wash. So what if Bryn had withheld the fact that he could dance? In the grand scope of things, it was minor. In her relationship with her eldest brother, it was life altering. Bryn had always been her most steadfast champion. Of her brothers, he tormented her the least and aided her the most.

He didn't deserve her surliness. None of her brothers did. They, the Peregrines, and even Lark, deserved better. Lark had taught Bryn to dance. Bryn, who'd never shown any romantic interest in a woman. Not until Lark, who'd won his heart and broken it.

She had to find out why. Bryn had always taken care of her. It was time for her to take care of him and make up for her antagonism. She lifted her gaze to find Max standing close beside her with a determined look on his face.

The familiar expression cheered her as much as one of his smiles or the sound of his voice or— When he opened his mouth to speak to her, her heart raced with anticipation.

"Don't go anywhere." Jack's order stopped whatever Max had been about to say.

He glared at his brother.

Oblivious to Max's crossness, Jack smiled at Birdie in the same adoring way she smiled at Jack as she said, "We have gifts to give."

Robyn forced herself to smile with them. *Don't be surly. Not to them. Not to anyone.* Her cheeks began to ache. Being polite and cheerful was as tiring as wearing a dress.

Jack pulled the red cloth bundle, which Birdie had carried from Peregrines' Post, from behind Birdie's bed. He set it on her lap and scooped her up, blankets and all.

Birdie's eyebrows arched in disbelief as he carried her to the closest person, who happened to be Max. "You don't have to cart me everywhere. Max could've come to us."

"He already has," Jack said. "He made the journey from Denver, and he still hasn't had his holiday."

Max snorted a laugh. "I can't fault you for seizing any reason or opportunity to hold your wife." His gaze went to Robyn, and a myriad of expressions flashed, too fast to identify, across his face.

Whatever he was thinking, he left her breathless.

"Max?" Birdie's voice drew his gaze from Robyn to Birdie.

She held out a multi-colored Christmas ornament swinging on a velvet loop.

When he held it on his palm, they both stared at the gift in confusion. Then she smiled again. At the gift's plump body, pointed nose and tail, beaded eyes, and teardrop-shaped...wings. Birdie's gift was a small bird made of fabric. An ivory bird with blue wings, wearing a jaunty yellow cap.

"Sorry we didn't have time to wrap them," Birdie said as she handed a bird to Robyn.

"We were still making them this morning." Jack carried his wife to Gus, and she gave him a bird from her bundle.

"Well, ain't they the sweetest little— Wait. Did you say *we?*" Gus challenged.

Jack grinned. "Your passion for new projects inspired me to also try something new."

Lark gasped when Birdie handed her a bird next. "You made one for me?"

"Of course." Birdie gave ones to Bryn, Hedd, and Griff as well.

"And she made them look good," Jack said proudly. "I made—" He laughed. "The biggest parts. Not that anything about them is big. But their bodies are at least easier to stitch than their tiny eyes and detailed wings and hats."

"I've never seen anything like them," Max murmured.

Neither had she. Everything about them was different. No two were the same. Or so she thought until she examined the birds everyone now held. The Llewellyns' birds wore red caps, while Max's had yellow and Lark's had black.

"The hats match our hair color." Max voiced her thoughts.

"But not mine." Gus sounded perplexed but still pleased. "Mine has a red and yellow and black hat."

"I bet you get all of our colors," Griff said, "because we all call you Grandpa."

"That's because he keeps telling us that we must," Hedd corrected quickly.

"And we are lucky that he does," Bryn remarked even faster.

"These hats look like..." Max's gaze met hers as if he was asking if she noticed what he was seeing.

She studied the birds closer. "They look like the wool caps you knitted for me and my brothers last Christmas!"

Birdie and Jack hadn't joined Gus' knitting activities as they'd assumed when the doctor mentioned a bed rest project. Instead, the pair had created their own miniature hats and birds to wear them.

"We made more to give out at the party." Birdie handed her the red bundle.

Why had she given them to her? When Jack set Birdie back on her bed, Robyn's answer became obvious. Birdie was on bed rest, and Jack wasn't going anywhere without her.

But Robyn had to keep her hands free and her thoughts focused if she wanted to succeed in getting Max to see all the ways she'd changed at tonight's party. She'd have to ask Hedd or Griff to give out the birds.

"There aren't enough for everyone in town." Birdie's chin rose determinedly. "So, we'll keep making them until everyone who wants one gets one."

"It's the least we can do for what they've done for us," Jack said. "We're blessed to live in this town. Mayor Hardt and the Noelle founders were wise men. Hardt's also a generous man. He inspired our Christmas ornaments."

"Dagnabbit." Gus slapped his knee. "I'd forgotten 'bout last year 'n the twelve ornaments. First the partridge, next the dove, and so on until the drum. They appeared like magic on the tree at the saloon." Gus grabbed the bundle from Robyn's hands. "I'll hand out yer birds at the party."

"*Merci, Grand-père*, but won't you have your hands full giving your own gifts? Surely someone else can do the task." Birdie's gaze swept Robyn's brothers.

Who exchanged odd looks, then stared at anything but Birdie.

"Fine," Robyn muttered when the situation was

anything but that. She reclaimed the bundle from Gus. "If *Bon-papa* is busy and no one else has the heart to volunteer, I'll do the job."

"No! You can't go to the party. That's not what we—" Hedd's gaze darted to his brothers, then to Max.

"You what?" she demanded.

"You look exhausted." Griff raised his palms placatingly when she scowled at him.

She forced her face to relax but couldn't resurrect her smile. She'd wanted to look her best for the party.

"We're all tired," Bryn said with a sigh. "And none of us are at our best when we are."

His word choice made her stiffen. Was it so obvious that she was failing at her plans?

"You shouldn't do things when you're angry, Rob," Griff muttered. "Believe me, I know."

"We should stay home for the evening so we can rest for our trip back to Denver early tomorrow." Despite his comment about slowing down, Hedd sped up and began pacing. "We'll have a lot of work when we return."

"We wouldn't have so much if you'd done *the one thing* I asked and stayed in Denver." Her accusing words made her growl in disappointment. Now she had more to make up for. "Stay here. I'm capable of attending a party on my own." She hugged Birdie's gifts to her chest. She might be capable, but she wouldn't be happy going alone.

"You ain't goin' on yer own," Gus said. "I'll be with you."

"And so will I," Lark declared.

Their support made her throat tight. Since she couldn't speak, she nodded her thanks.

"It'll be a fun gathering," Jack said. "Noelle's a good place to work and live. While you're mulling that over, Max and I need to talk about..." He trailed off as his gaze went to the front of the house. "What I wanted to discuss earlier. Let's talk outside."

Jack's secretive behavior made her head spin. So did Max's departure. He turned on his heel and, without a word, followed his brother down the hall.

CHAPTER 14

*W*hen they reached the porch, Jack sat down heavily on the steps and rubbed his thigh. Odd how his brother's wooden leg hadn't appeared to bother him that much when he'd carried Birdie, but now it did. Or maybe whatever he was about to say was the bigger bother. Jack wasn't rushing to reveal what he'd previously sounded so eager to tell Max.

He propped his shoulder against a post and stared at the sturdy ceiling. *I have nothing to say. I only want to speak with Robyn. I—* He shoved away from the post and started pacing. *I need to get back inside and talk to her.*

She was more determined than ever to go to the party. Her brothers had made her unhappy. Guilt pricked his heart. *I've made her unhappy.*

Jack blew out an extended breath. "I know your independence is important to you."

The unexpected words drained the gumption from Max's backbone and legs. He took a seat beside Jack on the steps. On the space his brother had left for him. *On purpose and with forethought. Darn him.*

Jack cleared his throat. "Which means you need to return to Denver. But I need to hand over our Noelle operations to someone."

Max stiffened, rejecting what had to be coming next. *You want me to stay in Noelle and run its office.*

"Birdie and I believe the best candidate to take over the Noelle office could be one of the Llewellyns."

Surprise made him turn to face his brother. "What?"

Jack raised his palms as placatingly as Griff had in the kitchen. "I know. Robyn's brothers messed up by abandoning their posts and coming here, but one misstep shouldn't negate all the good ones."

Max rubbed the knot tormenting his brow. "They'd always impressed me with their diligence and initiative in the past."

"So, our proposal is sound, but it isn't just our decision. It's a family one. And you know the Llewellyn family better than anyone. What do you think?" Jack clasped Max's shoulder. "Which one of the Llewellyns would be the best pick to stay in Noelle while you lead the rest in Denver?"

None of them. You can't part them. I can't either. No one can.

A dull ache throbbed behind his eyes. He couldn't say any of that to Jack when he looked so hopeful that his and Birdie's idea might work.

The blasted pain in his head swelled to the point where he felt like his world might explode. *Kaboom.* Like the bridge that'd been blown to smithereens and delayed the arrival of the— "Since the railroad reached town, your freight work has slowed down a lot, hasn't it?"

"It'll pick up again." Jack sighed wearily. "Noelle is growing more rapidly than ever. Folks will require more in-town shipping soon."

"But right now?"

"At most, it's a two-person job. Like when we first came to Noelle. One in the office and one on the wagon."

"Or a three-person job if one, like you, divided their time between the office and carpentry work."

Jack propped his elbow on his knee and his chin on his palm. "Or if one, like Gus, needed to slow down and enjoyed napping while watching the postal counter."

"You and him always knew the best way to handle the post." Max couldn't hide his grin. Jack always succeeded more than he failed at making sure Gus didn't work too hard.

"Lately he hasn't wanted to run the post office." Jack shrugged. "He's been interested in other things. Whatever Gus decides to do day-to-day, right now only two people can earn a steady income running Noelle freight. I wouldn't want anyone to move here and give up a lucrative position elsewhere. I'd worry less if everyone had a passion project they could fall back on in lean times."

"Like Gus has with his leather tooling—and you with your carpentry."

"And you had as well." When Max shot him a mystified look, Jack said, "Your knitting."

Max snorted. "That's not a job that'll put food on the table."

"Don't be so dismissive." Jack shook his finger at him. "It might."

"So might making Birdie's Christmas ornaments."

"True. But we'll never know about them because they're only a diversion. She'll want to return to her dressmaking soon." He glanced over his shoulder as if he might already find his wife creeping down the hall to work in her new dress shop.

"Too bad she couldn't do both." When Jack opened his

mouth to object, Max added, "I know. Birdie needs to slow down, and so do you. Those ornaments, however, might've been a great business opportunity."

Jack's worried frown turned confused. "How so?"

"We could've distributed them to the shops in Denver."

Jack huffed in disbelief. "You can see that *business opportunity*, but you can't believe those same shops might want your knitting?"

Max stared at the blindingly white but beautiful snowy vista around them. "Until now, I never gave anything but hauling freight my focus. It'd be an easy enough venture to test. We already know the steps after we distributed Birdie's dresses in Denver this year, and your wooden legs even further afield."

His brother smiled. "It's only an easy venture because you're in Denver. It was the best business decision you ever made, leaving Noelle and opening your office."

Jack's praise startled him. "It's your office as well." He raised a challenging eyebrow, then couldn't resist teasing his big brother. "Peregrines' Post is a family affair, you know."

Jack laughed and slapped him on the back. "And none of it would work so well if Denver was run by someone I *didn't know* and trust so completely."

"You know," Max repeated. "It's not just me making Denver a success."

"It's the Llewellyns," Jack replied without hesitation.

"They joined me during my first days." And what a gift that had been. He couldn't imagine not having Robyn in his life.

"So..." Jack climbed easily to his feet. Either the discomfort had faded from his leg, or he was ignoring it as he often did. "Assigning our Noelle office to one or two of the Llewellyns makes even more sense."

It did. And it didn't. Because Robyn's brothers had always insisted that their family was staying together. And if there was only work for two in Noelle, then he knew the Llewellyns' answer. They wouldn't and couldn't stay in Noelle.

Unless they were willing to learn new things. Like Jack had learned to make Birdie's ornaments, or Gus was knitting again. All four of the Llewellyns had never expressed an interest in doing anything other than driving wagons. Before, that single-minded interest had worked in Max's favor.

Now it was a disaster.

Because if the Llewellyns weren't capable of disbanding or diversifying, that meant his daily partnerships with them had come to an end. And so had his wish to share his future with Robyn.

His brother held out his hand. When Max grabbed it, Jack hauled him to his feet and said, "Time to see if Robyn and her family have stopped arguing and have time to talk to us. They seemed awfully riled about something." Jack gave him a knowing look. "*Something* bigger than a party."

Max led the way back to the kitchen and the Llewellyns. His stride was determined, but his head was bowed in defeat. "It's *something* I need to fix. In Robyn's favor."

CHAPTER 15

*R*obyn huffed, trying to blow one of the curls— that had escaped her braid—off her nose. She didn't succeed. So, she tried to brush away the dust covering her skirt—her entire skirt—instead. She didn't succeed there either.

Dandy. Just dandy. Now her hair and her dress were messier than ever. And she was more tired than ever. And probably looked it.

What would Max say if he saw her now? She'd seen him as they'd worked together during the move, but they hadn't spoken.

But now their group, minus Birdie, who was still on bed rest, was almost done moving the last of the upstairs furniture to the new house. She set Gus' brass carriage clock on the night table Jack had built for his grandfather and sighed in appreciation. And envy. The Peregrines were so lucky to have a permanent home for themselves and their treasures.

Gus paused his rifling through a trunk in search of what he'd called *his best shirt for a shindig* and patted her hand. "Why the glum face? Yer strong 'n resourceful 'n have yer whole life ahead of you." He winked at her. "And yer still my favorite Llewellyn."

"We heard that," Hedd said.

"How can we not," Griff grumbled. "We're all in the same room."

"Doing our fair share assisting our not so equal-minded Grandpa set up his palatial new abode." Bryn's words and sigh were so melodramatic he made everyone laugh.

"Don't worry." Gus' grin widened with anticipation. "You'll receive yer rewards at the party."

"We're not going." Hedd's refusal came fast.

"Of course you are," Gus shot back. "How else am I gonna introduce you to the finest bachelors 'n...bachelor ladies in Noelle?"

All three of her brothers looked as appalled as she felt whenever Gus brought up the topic.

"I know what yer thinking." Gus shrugged one shoulder. "There should be a better word fer an unmarried lady. Spinster ain't right. Neither is maiden."

"We're not attending any party." Griff's ill humor was fierce, but, like Robyn and her brothers, Gus had learned to either ignore or confront him.

"Why?" Gus' scowl transformed into wide-eyed incredulity. "Oh, yeah, nearly forgot. You big, strong lads need to stay home 'n *rest*."

The need for rest, and arguing about it, had grown exponentially since their Christmas feast. The nonstop advice was the most exhausting of all. *Do this. Or this and that.* But according to her brothers—*whatever you do, don't go to the party.*

As if sensing her turmoil, Gus gave her and each of her brothers a stern look. "Only yer sister has the grit to stay the course 'n see this day through." Gus squinted at the clock she'd set on his night table. "It's time. The party has started."

"It has? But I'm not ready. I'm a mess." Her entire body went rigid with anxiety. "I haven't—"

"You're perfect as always." Max stood in the doorway of Gus' room, looking beyond perfect. His thick blond hair and red-blond beard. His richly deep mahogany brown eyes. His smile...even if it looked a bit sad, which didn't fit his complimentary words and the certainty in his voice.

"Yes, Rob's perfect." Griff planted himself in front of Max. "While you, most definitely, are not."

"Why are you dragging your heels?" Bryn moved close to Griff.

Hedd did the same, and they formed a row of three facing Max. "Yeah, what happened to Dog Bone?"

"What are you talking about?" she demanded.

"Max?" Birdie's voice drifted down the hall. "What's taking you so long to bring Robyn to me?"

Max gestured for her to come with him. She hurried past her brothers and followed him. Inside the next room, Birdie perched on her bed, sewing more bird ornaments. Lark sat with her, cutting out fabric pieces, while Jack rearranged furniture.

Lark's willingness to help, along with her recently revealed talents for cooking and dance instruction, shattered all of Robyn's assumptions. If she'd been this wrong about Lark's character, what else had she failed to see? Or seen incorrectly?

Birdie and Lark put their ornament making aside.

"We'd better hurry if we are going to get you ready," Birdie said.

"We?"

"Lark and I." Birdie's gaze went to Jack, then Max, and

finally over Robyn's shoulder. "You need to leave the room, gentlemen."

Her brothers hovered behind her.

Jack kissed Birdie's cheek. "I'll be back after you're done and I get Grandpa organized." He headed for the door.

"I'll help you," Max said, but instead of following his brother, he turned to Robyn. His earnest look stole her breath. "Then I'll be waiting downstairs to escort you to the party."

"You can't do that." Bryn widened his stance.

When Hedd and Griff mimicked his posture, their row of three became a barricade, stopping Max from following Jack out of the room.

"Why can't he?" Robyn asked. "And this time you'd better answer my question."

"Because—" Bryn threw his arms in the air. "Escorting you is my job."

Griff gaped at his brother, then hollered, "Have you lost your mind as well?"

"None of us are going," Hedd shouted. "We decided this long ago."

While her brothers argued, Birdie motioned her forward. When they stood close, she handed her red cloth bundle, now sewn into a sack, to Robyn and whispered, "Do you remember me telling you about Agatha Boonesbury?"

She nodded. Birdie had only mentioned Agatha to Robyn, but not to her brothers. If they had known, their teasing would've been colossal. Gus had almost married the lady on the twelfth day of Christmas last January. In the final minute, the pair had called off their union. No one knew why.

Birdie kept her voice low. "When you see Agatha at the party, introduce yourself and ask her to hand out the birds. I should've thought of this sooner. I'd like for her to be included in our family gift giving. And for her and Gus to finally—"

"Aggie's gonna be there?" Gus' question, loud and clear and right beside them, made them jump.

They exchanged guilty looks as if they'd been plotting a crime.

"*Oui, Grand-père*," Birdie said in a soothing tone. "I suspect she will."

Gus crossed his arms stubbornly. "Then I'm *not* going there."

"But you've worked so hard to make your secret gifts," Birdie said.

"And you were so excited to attend the party," Robyn added.

Gus' gaze plummeted to the floor. "I can't face Aggie on my own."

Robyn grabbed his hand. "You won't have to. I'll be with you."

"But not all the time. Or even a tiny bit of the time. You'll be too busy dancin' with those eager bachelors."

"We can't say for sure if there'll even be any bachelors there." If none of them showed up, Robyn would rejoice rather than complain. All she needed was for Max to be there.

"Of course, they'll be there." Gus' back hunched. "Same as Aggie will."

"But how many? Maybe just a few." She could deal with that.

"There'll probably be a hundred!"

Robyn knew he was exaggerating, but his next comment sounded much too realistic.

"On yer first day here, you saw maybe only a quarter of 'em at Fina 'n Nacho's diner."

Robyn groaned.

"That's the solution," Bryn announced. "Rob must chaperone Grandpa Gus while I chaperone Rob."

"That's not her job," Max said in a frustrated tone. "Same as you pointing out that escorting Robyn isn't mine. I'll stay by my grandfather's side tonight. *I'll* be the one who won't leave him alone."

"You will?" Gus said in an amazed tone.

"I'd be my honor. But first—" Max faced her again. "Can I talk to you? Before anyone goes anywhere and does anything else? In private? Out on the porch?"

"If you do," Birdie said reluctantly, "there might not be time for us to style Robyn's hair and assemble her wardrobe."

"That's more important than talking." Max stepped back, retreating away from her.

"No," she said, following him. "It isn't. Not if—"

He held his raised palms between them. "But this is what you've wanted. This is what made you leave Denver. And if we can't talk now or even at the party, then...." He released one of the deepest and saddest sounding sighs she'd ever heard. "We'll talk afterward."

Hedd's breath hissed between his teeth. "That'll be too late."

"It's already too late. Too much has happened to stay our previous course." Max strode toward the door. "Let's go, Grandpa."

"Not so fast." Bryn and her brothers stood their ground, blocking his exit.

Her heart leapt with joy. They wouldn't let Max leave. They knew what she really wanted.

"Your grandfather needs to get ready for the party as well," Griff said.

His words left her blinking in confusion.

Gus looked just as bewildered as he said, "I do?"

"Where's that fancy shindig shirt of yours?" Hedd stepped aside, creating a break for Gus to pass through.

"Oh, yeah. It's in my room. It'll only take a moment to find." Gus took off down the hall, mumbling, "I hope."

"A moment is all we need." Bryn motioned for Max to follow him.

"We can talk fast," Hedd reminded everyone.

"Especially if we're downstairs away from all these—" Griff's glare swept Robyn and Birdie. "Upstairs distractions."

Robyn's gut rolled with hope and doubt. Her brothers had been behaving as oddly as Max since they all came to Noelle. What would they say to him? What would be his reply?

She prayed they finally agreed on something that worked in her favor and brought her and Max together.

CHAPTER 16

First his brother, and now Robyn's brothers. What was it with everyone wanting to talk to him when he only wanted to speak with Robyn? Once again, the Llewellyns stood in a row facing him. This time on the porch, where the air had gotten a lot frostier since his conversation with Jack.

"What're you doing?" Anger and disappointment twisted Bryn's face. "You're supposed to be stopping Rob's transformation, not accepting it."

"Or worse," Griff hissed. "Assisting it."

"You're acting like you've given up on our plan," Hedd accused.

"Of course, I have. That plan is over. I should never have agreed to it. And the only reason I chose to join you out here is to talk about a new plan."

Bryn cocked one eyebrow disdainfully. "To talk or to *tell?*"

"There's only one part to tell. I won't let—"

"You've never acted like a tyrant before," Griff growled.

"Yeah, and today ain't a good time to start," Hedd added.

"I won't wait for another time." Max crossed his arms. "I won't let you sabotage any of Robyn's plans. Not today, or ever again. The rest is open to discussion. You can get on board or—"

"Or we can get off." Hedd gestured toward the porch steps.

Bryn's good eye pierced him. "Remember, if Rob stays in Noelle, then *all three* of us are staying here as well."

Frustration made Max's voice sharper than he intended. "You can't."

"Stone the tyrant," Hedd hollered.

Griff roared even louder. "Drag him behind the wagon!"

Max threw his hands in the air. "If you stay in Noelle, you won't have enough freight work to support your family. There's not enough for *all four* of you."

"Are you firing us?" Griff demanded from between clenched teeth.

"No, I'm doing the opposite. I'm giving you—" He shook his head. "My family are giving you the reins of the Denver office."

The three brothers gaped at him in astonishment.

"The reins..." Hedd's voice faded before returning in a disbelieving whisper. "As in control?"

Max spread his arms wide. "Everything to do with that office is yours to run."

"And what will you be doing?" Bryn's question rumbled with suspicion.

He shrugged, trying to hide the bleakness that swamped him whenever he thought about being parted from Robyn. "I'm staying in Noelle."

Her brothers pressed closer to him and spoke so fast that he couldn't tell who said what.

"You're taking over your brother's office."

"So he can work at home with Birdie."

"But you'll be bored in Noelle."

He crossed his arms again and held his ground. "I'll have my work to keep me occupied."

Bryn spun away from him and sat on the steps. "Enough for one, but not for five."

His calculation humbled Max. He hadn't said four. He'd automatically included Max in the tally.

He took a seat beside Bryn, in the space Robyn's eldest brother had left for him. *I guess I have two big brothers now.* He coughed to clear the lump that rose in his throat. "Actually, Jack estimates enough for two. I'll have to hire someone to watch the Noelle office when I'm really busy."

Hedd and Griff leapt off the porch so they could stand at the foot of the steps and glare at him again.

"But—" Hedd sputtered. "But you love your office work best of all."

Griff's face turned red with outrage. "What did your brother *tell you* when you two were out here earlier?"

"I've already told you."

Bryn grunted. "Stop being stubborn."

His chest grew tight as he watched Bryn from the corner of his eye. "I thought I was determined."

Bryn smiled sadly. "It's often the same thing, Dog Bone."

The reinstatement of his name made his chest hurt even more.

"Tell us," Hedd ordered in a clipped tone. "Everything."

"Yes," Griff growled. "Tell us what your brother said. *Exactly.*"

Exactly? The word resurrected a memory. Not from his previous conversation with Jack, but with these men. Four days ago, he'd stressed the same word when he'd demanded that they tell him what Robyn had said, *exactly*, before leaving Denver.

He inhaled a long, slow breath. "Jack suggested that one or two of you take over the Noelle operations while the rest worked with me in Denver. He said the final decision—who stayed in Noelle—should be up to me because I knew you better than he did."

The following silence was disturbed only by the wind rustling the treetops and the even more muffled thumping of the silver mine in the distance.

Bryn released one of his familiar, deeply heavy sighs. "But you knew our thoughts on splitting up our family."

"We like what we have in Denver," Griff grumbled.

"No offense to Noelle," Hedd explained swiftly, "but it's too small for us."

His urge to defend Robyn's future, if even from afar, remained strong. "Maybe for you. I wouldn't be so sure what Robyn prefers anymore."

Griff's gaze rose to the second floor where Robyn was changing again. "She certainly hasn't enjoyed being with us lately."

"She's been awful chummy with the Noelle women," Hedd declared.

"They're good friends to have. When you get back to Denver, you must help Robyn make more friends there."

"And what about you and Rob?" Bryn asked.

"Yeah," Hedd said, "you and her are *best* friends."

"Maybe the only reason we are, or were, so close was because she hadn't the time to find new friends." The possibility sent a chill up his spine.

Griff shook his head violently. "That isn't true."

"How do you know?" Before they could answer, he said, "All I know for sure is that I can give Robyn the gift of a better future. Running her own business with her brothers, and not just working for me."

Hedd huffed. "We never worked *for* you."

"We worked *with* you," Bryn explained. "And that's why we liked it."

Me too. "But we all need jobs. Stable ones. And Robyn, more than anything including dancing, needs a home she won't have to pack up and leave again anytime soon." He set his jaw. "There's nothing more to say. So yes, it appears I'm telling you and not talking to you."

"There has to be another option," Bryn muttered. "You could hire someone else to handle all of the Noelle freight."

"My brother would never go for that. He'd give up his carpentry and go back to work at the office."

"But he was fine with one of us running things," Hedd objected.

"Because he trusts you," Max said.

"How can he?" Griff's tone was gruff with exasperation. "We were only in charge of Denver for a few days while you were away. And we failed you by coming here."

"Don't sell your contribution short. You've made that office prosper from the start and now you're like *family*." The word came easily, even if his relationship with the Llewellyn brothers took effort. But he'd never known easy. And maybe it was better this way. Their family bond was strong, and now so was his again.

"If we're family, we gotta stick together. There must be a way." Bryn looked to his brothers, who shrugged and appeared as unhappy as Max felt.

The door behind him opened.

Gus strutted out wearing a fancy shirt with ruffles at the collar and cuffs. "What're you doing sitting down? You gotta get ready for the party." Gus tossed him the suit he'd brought from Denver.

"How did you find—?" He shook his head. "Never mind. We need to get going."

"Yes sirree, we sure do." Gus' smile became a worried frown. "And remember, yer staying by my side all night."

He clasped his grandfather's shoulder. "While I'm helping you hand out your gifts, can you help me do something for Robyn?"

Gus stood straighter, like a sergeant ready for duty. "For Robyn, I'd do anything."

"I want to make sure she gets to dance with lots of partners, so she sees what her life could be and not merely what it has been."

Gus' grin returned. "I can do that."

"Good." He turned back to her brothers and their still unhappy faces. "Because Robyn deserves this opportunity to change, to try new things, and meet new people."

"And after the party?" Bryn asked.

"We all go back to work. You and Robyn in Denver. And me in Noelle." He forced himself to smile. Tonight, he'd be happy for her. And also to be in the same room with her. There'd be plenty of time to be miserable in the long days and nights that loomed ahead without her.

CHAPTER 17

*J*nside the Golden Nugget Saloon, Max followed his grandfather with one burlap sack over his shoulder and another held open in front of him. That gave Gus both hands free to pull out secret gifts for every person they passed while saying *Merry Christmas* in his jolliest voice.

Gus had achieved his goal. The gift recipients were all surprised. Some so much that they could only whisper a startled *thank you* or nothing at all. Gus took their reactions in stride as he distributed his, and Ezra's, and Jasper's creations. A single lumpy and misshapen sock.

Gus' nonstop advice-giving brought as much wonder as the knitted marvels.

"Don't have a wallet? Keep yer money in yer stocking," Gus suggested as he gave socks to Reverend Hammond and his wife, Felicity. When he handed more to Mayor Hardt and his wife, Penny, he said, "Keep yer feet warm 'n yer heart will be even warmer."

That one didn't work so well because Gus was only

giving one sock to each person. He and his team hadn't had time to make a pair for everyone.

Max winked at the mayor. "Maybe next Christmas Grandpa will have time to make you another stocking to match."

The man laughed as he clasped Max's hand. "Good to have you back with us, Max." His grip tightened as he pulled Max closer and whispered, "Say you'll save us all and stay to take over the knitting."

He shrugged noncommittally and continued following Gus.

The socks weren't that bad. Not for two absolute beginners and a third who only recently remembered how to knit. At least Gus remembered. For now.

And maybe Max would take up knitting again. He'd have to do something to fill every waking minute he stayed in Noelle. Otherwise he'd go crazy missing Robyn.

He didn't want to discuss his plans until he spoke to her. He'd wanted to tell her first, but the gathering at the new house had made that impossible. Now the crowd in the saloon kept crushing the hope that he'd be able to talk to her here.

A couple he'd never met before, but who introduced themselves as Romeo and Jane, gave Gus a beautiful stained-glass ornament while Gus gave them stockings. Whatever they said to each other was lost on Max when, on the other side of the saloon, a flurry of whispers that rivaled the stir Gus had first created drew Max's attention. And then made his heart race like a runaway wagon.

Robyn walked through the saloon door, graceful as a queen with three mighty knights and a fair maiden escorting her.

He stifled his urge to rush to her. With Bryn by her side

and Hedd and Griff trailing close behind with Lark ensconced between them, there was no room for him. He stayed close to Gus. As he'd promised. He couldn't stop his gaze from continually going Robyn's way.

In the candlelight, her hair glowed like a ruby sunset, while her feathered hat and silver-blue dress shimmered as beckoningly as stars on the horizon. Modern and regal. Modest and elegant. Birdie had outdone herself with tailoring this new garment's fitted waist, wide collar, and only slightly flared skirt to suit not only Robyn's tall, lean body but her red hair and steel-blue eyes.

Eyes he longed to see looking at him with the spark that always preceded her smile.

When she scanned the room, his heart thundered even faster, hoping she was searching for him. His hopes were dashed when, before her gaze reached him, she focused on a white-haired lady of Gus' age and made a beeline for her.

After a quick exchange of words, Robyn handed Birdie's red sack to the woman, and they shook hands. Robyn leaned closer to her new friend and whispered in her ear. The woman immediately pointed in his and Gus' direction.

"Dang it," Gus gasped. "She's spotted me."

"Less of a spotting," Max remarked, "and more of a knowing exactly where to look even before she was asked."

"My Aggie has eagle eyes," Gus muttered with affection and apprehension.

He should've guessed the woman's identity, Gus' one-time fiancée Agatha Boonesbury. He probably would have if he hadn't been so distracted by Robyn.

He watched spellbound as, after the briefest of glances his way, she turned to her brothers and Lark and said something that made them cluster around Agatha.

Heaven help them if they teased the lady about Gus.

He'd been warned off the subject by Birdie. When Agatha patted her hair and dress as if preening, he suspected they were complimenting her. The Llewellyn men must have learned something during their walk with Robyn and Lark to the saloon.

He'd truly miss their terrible teasing, but he'd miss the sight finally heading his way a thousand times more. Robyn had set a direct course for him.

The second she left her escorts' hulking shadows, Noelle's bachelors swarmed her. The first barely got in two words before a woman with reddish-brown hair and a determined expression tapped him on the shoulder and engaged him in conversation.

"Good to see the matchmaker continuing her righteous work," Gus said.

"But—" Max shook his head in disbelief. "She stopped that man from talking to Robyn. That's not good."

"Yer right, it's inspired," Gus proclaimed. "Genevieve Kinnison is a wise woman who's made matchmaking her trade. She brought the twelve brides to Noelle last Christmas. Without her, yer brother would've never married Birdie." Gus' voice turned gruff. "And I'd have never met Aggie."

Max's jaw dropped when the women who'd been in Peregrines' Post the day Birdie collapsed did the same thing as the matchmaker. They poked and prodded the bachelors into conversing with them and not Robyn. His stomach plummeted along with his hopes for Robyn to have a good time when the women's husbands did the same thing to every man who approached Robyn.

"They're ruining Robyn's evening," Max said in dismay.

"I'd say they're making it."

He huffed. "They're *making it* impossible for her to converse with new people and—"

"Possible fer her to do what she really wants. Spend time with you."

"You can't know that."

"I can 'n I do, Maximilian Boy. I see what our friends see. You 'n Robyn are meant fer each other. And this"—Gus gestured to the townsfolk's interference—"is Noelle's gift to the pair of you."

When both Culver and Ezra—who'd told him earlier that they owed him favors—gave him a salute and joined the throng distracting the bachelors, Max realized his grandfather was right.

"But you agreed to help me ensure Robyn danced with lots of partners and—"

Gus elbowed him in the side and whispered, "Wake up 'n pay attention to the treasure inside the gift wrapping."

When Robyn halted in front of him, he released the breath he'd been holding and let the happiness, that always surged in his veins when she was near, flow unrestrained.

Her eyes shone brighter than her dress, her hat, all of the candles in the room, and every star in the sky outside. But her smile looked sad.

"I'm sorry," he blurted.

Her smile disappeared completely. "For what?"

"For you not getting to experience this party as fully as you should."

"Balderdash," Gus said as his gaze went to Agatha. "We're both sorry fer not payin' proper attention to the ladies who brighten our lives."

Robyn grabbed Gus' hand. "Aggie said she hopes to speak with you tonight, *Bon-papa*."

"She did?" Gus' spine straightened. "She does?"

"Why did you two stop talking?" she asked Gus. When her gaze went from Gus to him, he wasn't so certain who she'd asked.

"Because," Gus muttered, "no bride needs a husband who can't remember how he messed up their union. Aggie 'n I were about to say our vows 'n then—" He groaned. "Well, I can't remember what happened."

Max forced himself to speak with a confidence he didn't feel. "And now you have the opportunity to start over, Grandpa." He hoped this was his chance for the same.

"I'll tell her—" Gus shook Robyn's hand, still holding his, excitedly. "No, I'll *ask* her to forgive me. And I'll give her a sock." Gus yanked the last sack from Max and set Robyn's hand in his instead.

His fingers instinctively tightened around hers. When hers did the same, he grinned like a fool.

"Fortune favors the bold, Maximilian Boy," Gus called over his shoulder as he strode toward Agatha—through a crowd where every man who'd tried to talk to Robyn remained engaged in a conversation with someone else.

But for how long?

He had to say the right words and quick. He ran his hand over his bearded chin and down his throat, seeking to ease the sudden dryness parching his throat. His fingers moved to his hair, trying to comb it. He hadn't had time to spruce up his appearance like Bryn had advised him to do back in Denver.

Robyn's gaze followed his movements before stopping dead center on his chest. "You look handsome in your suit."

Thank the Lord for Gus. Without him, Max might have forgotten to wear the darned thing.

When she continued to stare at his chest as if mesmerized, Max's gaze dropped to see what held her attention. He found his hand pressing her palm to his heart like a lovesick suitor.

"You're the shining star of the party," he blurted.

She flashed him a smile that made his world even brighter. "I don't know about that, but I find wearing this new skirt is manageable. Birdie calls it a divided skirt. I call it a pair of wide-legged trousers. I can handle that better than a dress." When she leaned closer to him like they were fellow conspirators, his breath stalled in his throat. "This is the perfect compromise."

"You're perfect, Red Bird."

"No, Red Beard. You are." The intensity in her voice startled him.

His free hand rose to smooth his beard. "I should've shaved."

"Don't even joke about that," she growled.

"I'm not. I was told that if I wanted to compete with the Noelle bachelors, I'd have to shave."

Robyn gasped. "You can't." She tried to yank his hand away from his beard, but when he pressed her palm to his face, they both froze. Except for her fingers. They hesitantly explored his beard, the line of his jaw, and almost touched his—

He shifted his jaw so her fingertips brushed his lips.

Her eyes flared and sparked like blue fire.

"You were saying?" He spoke only to have the excuse to move his lips against her fingers. "Something about my beard?"

"Oh. Yes. Well... If you really wanted to, you could shave it. You really shouldn't want to, though. Because then I won't have a reason to call you Red Beard."

"You could call me something else." *Like husband. We could wake up together every morning and—* He shook his head. None of that could happen. She was going back to Denver, and he was staying in Noelle.

A frown pinched her brow. "What's wrong?"

He pulled her hands away from his face and his heart. He held them in the space between them, but didn't let go. He'd have to soon. But not yet. "It's a good thing we had this talk because I'd have made a mistake if I had more time."

"Don't ever change," she whispered fiercely.

"But you wanted to—"

"And I ruined our friendship."

"You can change your clothing, your hair, how you talk, or even how much you talk to me, but you can *never* change the way I feel about you. You're my best friend. You always will be."

An ear-splitting screech cut off whatever reply she might have said. The screech came again and again. It sounded like someone was murdering a fiddle.

On the stage the townsfolk had set up for the entertainers, a man was doing just that.

"Poor little instrument," Robyn muttered.

He grimaced. "If its strings snapped, it'd be a merciful end."

Robyn snorted. "She'll snap him first."

The crowd parted to let the *she* in question through.

Lark, with Bryn in her wake, stormed like an avenging angel straight for the violin's cry for help. Her long black hair flew behind her like a flag guiding a warrior to battle.

"Now there is the woman I remember," Robyn said in a voice full of awe.

"I thought you didn't like her."

"If she hurts Bryn again, I'll hate her again. But you can't dislike this. Wait and see."

But when Lark reached the man torturing the instrument, and his audience, she froze as if suddenly afraid. Bryn didn't. He leapt onto the stage and yanked the fiddle from its abuser. Everyone dropped their hands from their ears and sighed in relief.

When Bryn held out the violin for Lark to take, she shrank back and covered her throat. Bryn's shocked expression turned fierce. He snarled something that at this distance couldn't be heard.

But Lark heard him. And despite Bryn's outrage, or maybe because of it, she smiled. Like she hadn't smiled in years and might never get the chance again.

She also climbed onto the stage, unassisted and uncoerced, and took the violin from Bryn. The instrument rejoiced in her hands. The music flowed and soared, as happy as a meadowlark in the springtime. Or a man and a woman in love.

Max clutched Robyn's hands tighter. The melody expressed how he felt with her by his side. Alive.

Robyn's sigh sounded forlorn. "Her playing has this effect on everyone."

He doubted it. If he hadn't fallen in love with Robyn, he wouldn't feel even a fraction of what he felt now.

"Lark's music speaks to lost souls, but she won't add singing to tonight's performance. Something's wrong with her throat." Robyn's eyes narrowed with the determination of someone who planned to find out exactly what. "She's amazing with the fiddle, but nothing compares to her talent with the hurdy-gurdy."

The hurdy-what? He bit back the question. Whatever it was, it wasn't as important as the scene unfolding around them. Everyone turned from the stage in search of dance partners. The bachelors stared at Robyn with renewed vigor.

Fortune favors the bold. We can't change the past. We can only change the future.

And he desperately needed one last memory with Robyn to get him through his future without her. "Will you show me how to dance again?"

He prayed the *again* part wouldn't ruin whatever happened next.

CHAPTER 18

$\mathcal{D}$ ancing with Max, standing so close and moving as one, Robyn had never been happier and sadder. This couldn't last. She fought the urge to clutch him tight and never let go. That wouldn't be ladylike. More importantly, that wouldn't give Max, or his family or hers, what they needed.

It'd just confuse the heck out of everyone since they'd more often than not watched her wiggle like a fish to escape embraces.

At least that had changed. From now on, she'd hug wholeheartedly. But she'd never dance with anyone again. Not after this. Not when she and Max moved so perfectly together.

"I need to tell you something." He sounded like he'd rather do anything but talk.

Here it comes. The big decision her brothers had warned her about during their walk to the saloon. What Max wanted to tell her was too immense. Too life-changing. Too heart-shattering.

Her mind scrambled for a different topic. A small one.

Which wasn't difficult. Every subject felt like a tiny snowflake under the cloud of what he would tell her. And what she must tell him.

Later. Right now, she wanted to pretend they could spend all of their tomorrows dancing and making each other smile.

"Why didn't you tell me that, like Brynmor, you could've taught me to dance in Denver?" she asked.

The startled look in his eyes narrowed with apprehension. He'd known this question was coming.

"Because I haven't danced in a while. I wasn't sure I'd remember the steps."

"You're an even better dancer than Bryn." Her compliment didn't make him smile like she'd hoped.

"I doubt that. Your brother learned not very long ago. I learned a *very long* time ago. So, if I'm any good, it's because you're my partner."

His praise made her grin. And when she did, he did too.

"Who taught you?"

His expression turned somber. "My grandmother."

"I wish I could've met her."

"Me too."

"Gus and Jack said she taught you to knit as well. There are so many things we've yet to discuss." Her throat tightened. *And our time is running out.*

"You're not upset that we didn't discuss this sooner? Like you were with Brynmor?"

She shrugged. "We all have reasons for doing things. Or not doing them."

"I would've gladly attempted to teach you to dance. In Denver, if I'd known you wanted to learn back then. Or here in Noelle had I"—he frowned and exhaled a long, resigned breath—"had the courage to broach the subject." He squared his shoulders as he muttered, "Fortune favors the bold."

Their reprieve was over. Their dancing became stiff. Their steps faltered.

"I've decided to stay in Noelle and run its office." His words came in a flurry, as if he worried that if he didn't talk fast, he wouldn't be able to speak at all.

Seeking to steady him and herself, she laid her palm against his face and his beloved red beard. "I know."

"You do? How?"

She raised her brows slowly. "How do you think?"

"Your brothers told you." His muscles relaxed, then sagged with defeat.

She felt her body do the same. She forced her shoulders as straight as his had been a moment ago. "And then I told them something." It was time to tell Max as well. "I'm staying in Noelle so you can return to Denver and the office you've worked too hard to give up."

"No." He shook his head fiercely. "No, you can't."

She trapped his face between her hands and held him still. Unfortunately, that meant they stopped dancing. At least he was looking at her and hopefully also listening to her.

"I can," she said softly and then firmly, "and I will. It's my choice."

He squeezed his eyes shut, rejecting her decision. The same as she'd rejected his.

But he also leaned into her touch like he couldn't stand without her. "There's not enough work for you and all of your brothers in Noelle."

"That's why two of them will go with you, and one will stay with me. And they'll routinely trade locations so we both get to spend time with each of them."

Max's breath hissed between his teeth like she'd punched him in the gut. "But not with each other. They agreed to this?"

"Yes, unless..."

His eyes opened and watched her warily. "Unless what?"

"My brothers have become very confusing men."

The line of his jaw hardened under her hands, but a smile also twitched his lips. "What I find works best is if I hear what they said *exactly*."

"They said: *Unless Dog Bone can make a different proposal*." She felt her cheeks flush as she said the word proposal.

The heat that flared in his eyes made her entire body burn.

"They rambled on about choosing with our hearts and nothing else." She growled in frustration, knowing she was also rambling. "They apologized profusely for being tyrants who always tried to tell me what to do. Which is peculiar because what they said made me feel like they were now telling me *and you* what to do."

The strength of his smile combined with the intensity of his gaze stole her breath. "When you look at me like this," she whispered, "it feels like all my dreams have come true."

"I'm ready to make my proposal." Neither his expression nor his voice wavered as he spoke. "My heart's choice is that you and I work together forever."

"You proposing"—the uncertainty that welled up inside her throat made it hard to speak—"a business venture?"

"Red Bird, is there anyone in this room that you'd still like to try dancing with?"

"No, of course not." She scowled at him. "There's only you."

"Then this is my proposal." He dropped down on one knee. "Will you marry me?"

"Yes!" She knelt with him and flung her arms around his neck.

His breath heated her ear as he whispered, "How about marrying me, right here and now?"

She gasped in delight. "This is where the twelve brides and grooms were married last year. And Reverend Hammond is here tonight. He could marry us *right now*."

They both scrambled upright and searched for him.

When she saw him across the room, she waved like a madwoman or the happiest woman on earth, trying to get his attention. When he didn't look her way, she put her fingers to her lips and released a shrill whistle.

Lark's violin playing halted. So did the dancing and all the conversation.

"Reverend!" they both shouted, then grinned at each other.

Despite her overwhelming happiness, she shook her head at her behavior. "That wasn't very ladylike of me," she muttered to Max.

"But it was you. And me. Being ourselves." He raised his chin and yelled even louder this time, "Reverend, we'd like you to marry us."

"Right now," Robyn hollered.

A cheer went up. Suddenly, her brothers were slapping Max on the back. And Gus, followed by Agatha and Jasper and Ezra, were hugging her. And she was hugging them back.

Bryn's big arm looped around her shoulders and drew her close to his side. "I guess Dog Bone has finally decided who's staying in Noelle."

"We both decided." Robyn laughed as she surveyed the smiling faces of their family and friends clustering 'round them. "We *all* decided."

Griff frowned. "I'm gonna hate not seeing you every day, Little Red."

"But at least," Hedd said, "she'll talk to us when we do see her."

Max's smile remained steadfast. "You'll always be welcome to visit us in Noelle."

"But only one Llewellyn brother at a time." Hedd waved his index finger in the air.

"This time I'll make sure," Griff vowed, "that at least one of us is always holding the reins in Denver."

Like a quake rattling a mountain, Bryn's sigh shook his chest and Robyn as she leaned against him. "*This* might be the last time the Peregrine and Llewellyn families are all together."

His observation filled her with melancholy and dismay. "Jack and Birdie aren't here. We can't get married without them."

Reverend Hammond finally reached them. He beamed as happily as his wife, who held his arm. "So it's time for another wedding, is it?"

"Only if you can—" She spun to face Max.

When he held out his hand to her, Bryn released her, and she went eagerly into his embrace.

Max finished what she'd been about to say. "Can you marry us at Jack and Birdie's new house?"

"I can." The reverend chuckled. "But can you *wait* to get there? You seem awful impatient."

"If you all jumped in a wagon," Jasper suggested, "you'd get there faster."

"We didn't bring one," Gus grumbled. "We weren't in a rush when we walked here."

"Not everyone walked." Agatha stood close to Gus. "There are several wagons outside."

"You should take ours," Ezra told Max. "You've already had practice driving our team, so they should get you home extra fast."

"I'm the fastest." Hedd strode toward the door. "So I should drive."

Robyn and Max beat him to the driver's seat. They claimed it together and sat side-by-side. Hedd didn't argue. Instead, he made a gallant show of assisting Agatha, much to the lady's delight, into the back of the wagon—while Bryn and Griff helped Lark and Gus get in.

While they did, the crowd that had followed them outside and now stood on the walkway, called out their best wishes for their marriage and the season.

"Merry Christmas!" she whooped as she yanked off her feathered hat and threw it to them.

One of the few single ladies in town caught the hat. Felicity and the matchmaker named Genevieve immediately linked arms with the woman and guided her back toward the saloon.

"Don't dawdle," Genevieve instructed the reverend, who was climbing into the wagon.

"You never know, husband dearest," Felicity added before the trio disappeared through the door, "when someone else might demand to be married in Noelle's saloon."

Max lifted the lines. "I'll knit you a new hat to replace the one you gave away."

"If you wish, but I don't need anything new." She pulled his wool cap from her skirt pocket, donned it, and grabbed his hand.

Griff snorted. "You can't hold hands and drive at the same time."

"Yeah," Hedd agreed, fast as a bolt of lightning. "You gotta decide. Who's driving this wagon?"

"We both are." Max placed one of the lines in her free hand and kept the other in his. "Ready?"

Her blood raced in her veins, anticipating what came next. "Always."

They both used their line to turn the wagon onto the road. Then they snapped their wrists in unison and urged the horses into a trot.

Max shifted closer to her on the wagon seat so that from ankle to hip to shoulder they touched. He'd removed the last distance between them. "I'll build you a house."

She smiled at their clasped hands resting on his knee. "I'll be there every day building it with you."

Behind them, Griff asked in an unusually hushed tone, "Will you have room for family?"

"Of course," Max and Robyn said at the same time.

"Then it's only right that we help with your new house," Hedd announced.

"You should build it beside Jack and Birdie's," Reverend Hammond added.

"Good idea." The vigor in Griff's voice had returned. As her youngest brother, he was used to being in the middle of things. He, more than anyone, would make sure the Peregrines and Llewellyns stayed together. "That way Busy Bee won't have far to go when he leads the construction."

"I'm also good at supervisin'," Gus proclaimed.

Agatha huffed. "You can do more than that."

"I can?"

Agatha's sigh sounded more amused than weary. "Must I remind you of everything?"

Gus chuckled. "I think that'd be best."

Robyn peered over her shoulder so she could scan the

dear souls who occupied the wagon bed and would soon attend her wedding. "Our plans are all set."

Except for Bryn and Lark. They continued to say nothing as Bryn stared at Lark, and she stared into the dark surrounding the wagon. Because Lark's songbird sisters were still out there. Somewhere. And she must soon continue her search for them.

And Robyn knew that Bryn wouldn't want her to go alone, and that Lark wouldn't want him to follow her and get hurt again. So Lark would probably leave Bryn again. In the dead of the night, if need be. That eventuality made Robyn's heart ache for both of them.

"The next turn's coming up," Max murmured.

She faced forward and adjusted her line in unison with his.

"We'll figure something out." Max's voice rumbled with his familiar determination. "And while we're doing that and building our new home, we'll have room at the office for your brothers *and* their friends. Friends who might be lucky like us and become more than friends one day."

With a bit of luck and a lot of love, there might be many blessings in their future. "I'm sorry I didn't get you a Christmas present this year."

"But you have." Max's smile raised hers as easily as a bird on a mountain wind. "You've given me your time and your hand in mine."

"And so have you." Her grin grew even wider. "Of all the gifts in Noelle, these are the wisest."

"Are you sure?" A teasing glint entered his eyes. "I think we've forgotten one." The spark in him became a flame as his gaze locked on her mouth. "One that usually comes after a wedding. But why wait?" He leaned toward her.

She met him halfway and added a first kiss to their gifts
—with a promise of many more to come.

Thanks for reading *Robyn: A Christmas Bride!*
I hope you enjoyed Robyn and Max's adventure—and Gus,
Jack, and Birdie's continuing stories as well.
If you haven't read their first Christmas book (set a year
earlier when 12 mail-order brides come to Noelle), look for
The Calling Birds.

To learn what happens after Robyn and Max's story, keep
reading to see an excerpt from
A Bride for Brynmor, where...while searching for her sisters
in Denver, Lark runs into her troupe manager, Ulysses T.
Stone, instead.

See the next plage to learn where to leave a review of *Robyn:
A Christmas Bride* and how deeply reviews are appreciated...

DEAR READER

I hope you enjoyed Robyn and Max's journey to find their home together in the town of Noelle.

If you did, please consider writing a review or say hello via the usual places, including email. Every single review helps. No matter how long or short, they are a heartfelt gift that is sincerely appreciated.

Hearing from readers makes my day and keeps me motivated to write my next book. Looking forward to hearing from you!

Review on AMAZON
www.amazon.com/author/jacquinelson
www.amazon.com/dp/B07LGVLXS8

Review on GOODREADS
www.goodreads.com/jacquinelson

Review on BOOKBUB
www.bookbub.com/authors/jacqui-nelson

STORY INSPIRATION

When I started pondering a plot for my Christmas story, my first question was, what should the theme be? Is there a classic Christmas tale with an uplifting theme that many people might recognize or at least relate to? *The Gift of the Magi* became my first inspiration when writing *Robyn: A Christmas Bride.*

The Gift of the Magi (written by O. Henry and published in 1905) features the themes of selfless gift giving and how the gift of love is priceless. In that story, a husband and wife each sell their most valuable possession, but they are items that can be grown again (hair) or can be bought back again (a watch). I wondered what if the thing you valued most was sustaining a way of life that you'd struggled a long time to create and that now defined your entire self-worth? Could you give that up if it meant ensuring the happiness of a loved one? That might be the ultimate selfless gift to give.

My next thought was having a heroine who was a trouser-wearing tomboy who loved driving wagons in 1877, a time when society wasn't very accommodating about women's appearances and occupations that strayed from the norm. So...what if my heroine decided she needed to do something drastic to win the heart of the man she loved? Changing yourself to please another person (even if they haven't asked you to) might be considered another selfless gift. So...what is a classic transformation story? *My Fair Lady* and its heroine, Eliza Doolittle, were my next inspiration.

My Fair Lady (released in 1964 as a movie starring Audrey

Hepburn) focuses on speech lessons, but Eliza's transformation also includes her appearance—her clothing, hair, the way she carries herself, and more. It's a life-changing transformation that is difficult for Eliza and takes hard work and sacrifice—for her own good (a chance at better job prospects) but also, as time goes on, to please her instructors.

So...selfless giving and self-sacrifice. Ready. Set. Go. Write a Christmas story.

I hope you enjoyed *Robyn: A Christmas Bride* as much as I enjoyed not only writing the story but also giving Robyn Llewellyn and Max Peregrine their hard-won and well-deserved Christmas gifts.

~ Jacqui

A BRIDE FOR BRYNMOR - EXCERPT

The story that follows *Robyn: A Christmas Bride* (also book 1 in the *Songbird Junction* series, a Llewellyn Brothers Western Historical Romance)

≈

Can a sister who's lived only for others find freedom with one man?

Family has always come first—for both of them. He's never forgiven himself for letting her go. She's never forgiven herself for almost getting him killed.

When Lark and her songbird sisters are separated fleeing their cruel and controlling troupe manager, only Brynmor Llewellyn can help Lark save her sisters and escape to the far west. But Lark wants more. And so does Brynmor. When they're stranded in a spot as difficult to guard as it is to leave —a rustic cabin at a train junction between Denver and the mountain town of Noelle, Colorado—they find themselves fighting not only for survival but for redemption, forgiveness, and a second chance for their love.

Will the frontier train stop of Songbird Junction be Lark and Brynmor's salvation? Or their downfall when her manager, a con artist who calls himself her uncle but cherishes only his own fame and fortune—demands a debt no one can pay?

≈

CHAPTER I

January 1878
Denver, Colorado

Alone in the shadows of the alley, Lark surveyed the sunny street filled with city folk who might end her family's escape if they— She shook her head, rejecting her doubt. *If* wasn't acceptable. She couldn't fail her sisters again.

Oriole and Wren *had* to make it to their pre-arranged meeting place across the street.

She tucked her nose under her scarf, thrust her hands deeper into skirt pockets, and rocked on her boots. Nothing helped. Her shivers grew because they weren't from the frosty air or the snow-covered ground.

She trembled with dread that her pursuit of freedom might end in her sisters' deaths.

Oriole, sweet as she was savvy, had chosen this location. But two years earlier, when Oriole's violin required repairs, Oriole had been the only one allowed to enter Mrs. Fitz-patrick's Music Emporium.

Lark had been disappointed not to view the treasures inside. Today, she cared only for what she might see outside —her sisters, who'd agreed to meet at the music shop if they were separated fleeing Cheyenne. After sixteen years together, the last twelve days apart made her heart ache unbearably.

She kept searching for Wren's tiny and timid form—so easily lost in a crowd. And smothered there as well. Being a head shorter and a couple of years younger than Lark and Oriole hadn't helped Wren's confidence either.

Wren may be the best singer in their three-woman songbird troupe, but she only shone when she performed in the circle of their act. Wren would suffer the most on her own.

How could she have lost them? She'd lied and schemed and surrendered everything to keep their trio together, including her liberty and the man she loved. How had it all gone so wrong?

Because Beelzebub wouldn't let his pawns go without a fight.

Their troupe manager, Ulysses T. Stone, was both a devil and a dog. He had a hound's nose for finding people he could bamboozle into giving him what he craved most: fortune and fame. He coveted an audience's attention as much as their money.

Anger stirred the turmoil in her heart. He may be the maestro of manipulation, but she was the granddaughter of Cree warriors. She would not fail Oriole and Wren. She would find them and take them far away from the man who'd vowed to never let them go.

She scanned the street for the wiry, dark-haired Irishman whose fake gentleman's accent and dandified clothing concealed a thug carrying an arsenal of weapons, including a spring-loaded derringer under one ruffled sleeve. No one, in disguise or plain sight, matched his stature.

She saw no sign of Oriole or Wren either. They'd agreed to meet at noon. Her pocket watch read five past one.

Accept it. There's no when or if. They aren't coming.

Or maybe they'd arrived earlier and gone? But not before leaving a message saying where. They'd agreed to do that as well.

Abandoning her hiding spot, she crossed the street at a brisk pace. The snow crunching under her feet marked her progress as she slipped into the alley flanking the music shop and examined the wall from top to bottom. When she rounded the back of the building, she found that alley empty as well. A stroke of luck.

She continued hunting for a crevice that held a piece of paper. There had to be a letter. Had she missed it? If she did a second pass, maybe she'd—

"Looking for something?" The words cracked like a whip, close behind her.

Cringing from the memory of his lash on her back, she spun to face Ulysses. The footlong strip of rawhide tied to his wrist remained lowered. A weapon she now feared had permanently scarred the one good Samaritan who'd been brave—and foolhardy—enough to step between her and her troupe manager.

∽

To read more about *A Bride for Brynmor*, visit JacquiNelson.com

Hope you'll add *A Bride for Brynmor* to your "want to read" shelf on Goodreads at Goodreads.com/jacquinelson

SONGBIRD JUNCTION SERIES

The Llewellyn Brothers
Western Historical Romance Trilogy

Welcome to SONGBIRD JUNCTION, where Welsh meets West in Colorado, 1878. The journey to find a forever home and more starts here...

Brynmor, Heddwyn, and Griffin Llewellyn are three Welsh brothers bound by blood and a passion for hauling freight —in Denver, where hard work pays.

Lark, Oriole, and Wren are three Irish-Cree Métis sisters-of-the-heart bound by choice and a talent for singing—in any place that pays.

Will the frontier train stop of Songbird Junction be their families' salvation? Or their downfall when the sisters' troupe manager—a con artist who calls himself their uncle but cherishes only his own fame and fortune—demands a debt no one can pay?

Claim your ticket to travel from America's booming small-towns to the most promising train junction in the Rocky Mountains' snowbound wilderness where—during three perilous quests for freedom, truth, and harmony—the final destination will always be true love.

FREEDOM. TRUTH. HARMONY.

Bride for Brynmor - Book 1
Can a sister who's lived only for others find
freedom with one man?

A Bride for Heddwyn - Book 2
Can a sister who's lied to everyone find
truth with the wrong man?

A Bride for Griffin - Book 3
Can a sister who's lost her voice find
harmony with the right man?

PRAISE FOR THE SONGBIRD JUNCTION SERIES...

A Bride for Brynmor
Songbird Junction, Colorado - January 1877

"A special journey that kept me following along to see what would happen. I cannot wait to read about the other two sisters and also Brynmor's brothers turn out!" ~ Lori D.

"A perfectly written love story." ~ SKM

"Oh, I love this book. There is something about getting lost for a few hours in this era. So well written and descriptive, you feel like you are right there in all the action." ~ B

"A great love story with perilous danger." ~ Dorothy R.

A Bride for Heddwyn
Songbird Junction, Colorado - January 1877

"A splendid cast of characters...a book that will be re-read over and over again." ~ Crystal Crossings

I loved this couple. Heddwyn is perfect for Oriole and she for him." ~ Cheryl P.

"Throw in a cute puppy, a troop of gypsies, & meddling family, and the charming adventure is complete" ~ Michelle R.

"Mayhem, both funny and heart warming." ~ Betty R.

THE CALLING BIRDS - EXCERPT
The Fourth Day in the
Twelve Days of Christmas Mail-Order Brides series

*A wanted woman's flight,
a man in pursuit of honesty, not stolen gold...
and only nine days left to save the town.*

Many years have passed since **Bernadette Bellamy** fled the Cariboo Gold Rush and her reputation as the sister of a French-Canadian gang of thieves. Armed with only an honest talent for sewing and a willingness to lead a solitary life on the run, she stays one step ahead of everyone seeking her brothers' last—and now lost—heist. Until a craving to settle down makes her reinvent herself as **Birdie Bell**, a dress shop owner. The arrival of an old foe combined with her desire to hold onto her treasure trove of fabrics has Birdie joining a wagonload of brides bound for a remote town.

After losing his leg and his wife, **Jack Peregrine** buries his pain under a mountain-high pile of work. He only agrees to sign up for a mail-order bride to save the town of Noelle, keep his freighting business, and care for his absentminded grandfather. But Jack's request for a sturdy bride who won't crumble under his burdens brings him a woman as tiny as she is troubled. Can two mismatched people band together to become the perfect match?

THE CALLING BIRDS

Noelle, Colorado
December 24, 1876

A crowd of women filled *La Maison's* front hall. One of them was Jack's bride, Birdie Bell. A hard-working woman who'd started her own dressmaking business in Denver. A mature woman of thirty. A strong woman who wouldn't break under life's hardships.

Maybe his luck would change today. With time Miss Bell might come to respect or maybe even enjoy his company. He needed this marriage to last.

He should've looked for his grandfather first, but he couldn't stop his gaze from scanning the women in search of his bride. Even wild-swept from the storm and huddled together shivering from the cold, the women were a fine-looking bunch. How had Mrs. Walters managed that?

A raven-haired, pale-skinned woman standing slightly apart from the rest snared his attention. Her beauty would've been enough to hold any man spellbound, but her tiny size turned him rigid with concern. A woman so small wouldn't last long in a town like Noelle.

His worry turned to anger. Whoever had asked her to come here should be horsewhipped!

A faint smile curved her mouth, as if she was amused by the prospect of being housed in a location as scandalous as La Maison. He must be dreaming. She shouldn't be here, and she couldn't be amused.

She surveyed the room, studying everything and everyone—until she saw him. Then she stared at him the way he felt he must be staring at her, as if mesmerized.

"I've come for a bride," a voice proclaimed loudly, a familiar voice that made him cringe. "Which one of you is the future Mrs. Peregrine?"

The woman spun to face the speaker—his Grandpa Gus.

A wave of gasps and tittering laughter swept through the crowd. Several of the women glanced at the tiny woman who'd captivated him. She was now staring at Gus with wide eyes.

Her gaze darted to him. When she caught him still staring at her, her expression turned blank and devoid of emotion. She straightened her shoulders, strode straight up to Gus, and said in a lyrical voice with a seductively foreign accent, "I am the bride you seek, Mr. Peregrine. My name is Birdie Bell."

A surge of euphoria followed quickly by alarm made him stagger and lean heavily against the nearest wall. This tiny Frenchwoman couldn't be Miss Bell. He'd asked for a strong woman. This one wouldn't be able to hold up under his workload, the rough town, or the surrounding wilderness. She'd abandon Noelle and him.

Could he blame her if she did?

If she didn't, she might die here.

"No!" His voice shot out louder than Gus' a moment ago.

Complete silence descended around him. The chance to make a good impression was long gone. Everyone in the front hall stared at him, including his tiny bride.

To read more about *The Calling Birds*, visit JacquiNelson.com

If you haven't already, don't forget to add *The Calling Birds* to your "want to read" shelf on Goodreads at Goodreads.com/jacquinelson

Deadwood, Dakota Territory 1876...
In a gold rush storm, can an unlikely pair rescue each other?
Raven wants to save one person. Charlie wants to save the
world. Their warring nations thrust them together but duty
pulled them apart—until their paths crossed again in
Deadwood for a fight for love.

EXCERPT
RESCUING RAVEN - CHAPTER 1

Fighting a growing impatience fueled by rage, Charlie
Jennings drew his revolver and urged his horse through the
trees flanking the Deadwood Trail. Below him, an
Appaloosa with the strikingly similar color of his own horse
—white covered from head to hock in chestnut spots—was
rein-tied to the back of a buckboard. If the horse hadn't
caught his attention, he might not have given the transport a
second look.

He might not have seen her.

The wagon rattled forward carrying one silent and seven
grumbling passengers. When a bend in the trail cast the sun
in the eyes of the guards, one riding behind and the other in
front, he charged his spotted mare down onto the road.

Everyone in the wagon, except for the cowering raven-
haired woman, screamed. The driver jerked on the lines.

The horses skidded to a halt. The guards scrambled for their weapons.

The click of his revolver being cocked made them all freeze.

The silence that followed was as heated as the summer sun on his back. The guards glared at him through squinted eyes. He kept his focus on them as well—lined up in a neat row down the barrel of his Colt Peacemaker.

"Jennings," growled the closest man, who went by the name Big Bill. "You shouldn't be here."

"Yeah," hollered Bill's partner, a stranger who resembled a beanpole.

Frontier trails and towns had a way of attracting similarly named men, including the Charlies like him. They also had a fondness for embellishment. The deck was stacked in favor of the rear guard being called Skinny Sam or Loud-mouth Pete.

"We heard you were guidin' a miner 'n his four kids, the ones who lost their ma, away from Deadwood." At least Skinny hadn't heard, and used, the double-barreled moniker Charlie had been saddled with since arriving in the Black Hills.

"But you," he shot back, "didn't hear that my job finished ahead of schedule."

"Well," Bill said on a long breath, "ain't that a spot of bad luck."

"Not for one of your passengers." He didn't look her way. He'd already seen enough: a ragtag assortment of women, one hunched with her dark head over her wrists tied to the wagon.

To read the rest of *Rescuing Raven*, visit my website JacquiNelson.com and sign up for my newsletter.

ALSO BY JACQUI NELSON

SONGBIRD JUNCTION SERIES

A Bride for Brynmor - Book 1

A Bride for Heddwyn - Book 2

A Bride for Griffin - Book 3

The Llewellyn Brothers and Songbird Sisters trilogy is set in Colorado, 1878, and feature characters from my two Noelle, Colorado, Christmas stories.

∽

NOELLE, COLORADO

The Calling Birds: The Fourth Day - Christmas, 1876

Featuring characters from *Choosing Bravery*

Robyn: A Christmas Bride - Christmas, 1877

Featuring characters from *The Calling Birds*

∽

LONESOME HEARTS SERIES

Between Heaven & Hell - Book 1, Oregon Trail, 1850

Following Faith - Book 2, Oregon, 1852

Choosing Bravery - Book 3, Oregon, 1868

Rescuing Raven - Deadwood, 1876, a FREE read for my newsletter subscribers

∽

GAMBLING HEART SERIES

Between Love & Lies - Book 1, Dodge City, 1877

Between Home & Heartbreak - Book 2, Texas, 1879

∾

STEAM! ROMANCE AND RAILS

Adella's Enemy - Kansas, 1870

∾

To learn more about my books, visit my website

JacquiNelson.com

ABOUT THE AUTHOR

Fall in love with a new Old West... where the men are steadfast and the women are adventurous. You'll find Wild West scouts, spies, cardsharps, wilderness guides, and trick-riding superstars in my stories. Those are my heroines. Wait till you meet my heroes!

My love for historical romance adventures with grit and passion came from watching Western movies while growing up on a cattle farm in northern Canada. I've been nominated for over 20 awards and won the RWA® Golden Heart® & the Laramie® — but my best reward is hearing from readers who have enjoyed my stories.

Email me at Jacqui@JacquiNelson.com

For updates on giveaways, special events, and more, join my newsletter at JacquiNelson.com